TIME LIMIT

"I'm not for hire to *any* dope pushers," Tommy Lee said. "I don't give a damn if it's syndicate creeps or some hungry punks that have my skin color. The best thing that could ever happen was if you blew each other's brains out. Have a nice bloodbath, gentlemen—I'm leaving."

Before he could take a step to the door Bartlett Delmonico said, "you've got exactly forty-eight hours to find that gang and put them out of action or you'll be responsible for the deaths of a lot of innocent people."

"How do you figure that?"

"In exactly forty-eight hours we'll start taking three random hostages everyday from the streets of Chinatown and shoot them down. You get us what we want, Lee, or we'll start killing off your people!"

WRITE FOR OUR FREE CATALOG

If there is a Pinnacle Book you want but can't find locally, it is available from us—simply send the title and price plus 25¢ to cover mailing and handling costs to:

PINNACLE BOOKS
275 Madison Avenue
New York, New York 10016

__Check here if you want to receive our catalog regularly.

__Check here if you wish to know when the next_____will be published.

THE CHINATOWN CONNECTION
OWEN PARK

PINNACLE BOOKS   NEW YORK CITY

This is a work of fiction. All the characters and events portrayed in this book are fictional, and any resemblance to real people or incidents is purely coincidental.

THE CHINATOWN CONNECTION

Copyright © 1977 by Lyle Kenyon Engel

All rights reserved, including the right to reproduce this book or portions thereof in any form.

An original Pinnacle Books edition, published for the first time anywhere.

ISBN: 0-523-40-010-6

First printing, February 1977

Cover illustration by George Bush

Printed in the United States of America

PINNACLE BOOKS, INC.
275 Madison Avenue
New York, N.Y. 10016

THE CHINATOWN CONNECTION

CHAPTER ONE

Late this night in the dense, chokingly thick fog that covered San Francisco's Chinatown, darker shadows of evil were skulking in wait for a rich green prey—to rob, to maim and to kill like some monstrous new tribe of jungle beasts....

It was the kind of heavy, moist fog that had given San Francisco its legendary reputation for shrouded mysteries lurking in dim alleyways. The 2:15 a.m. Pan-American flight arrival from Hong Kong crept in over the bay with runway headlights fighting the murk every inch.

Once the half-full passenger load was processed through U.S. customs, it took the taxi hailed by the two oriental men nearly an hour to creep up the expressway into central San Francisco. The cab moved up Broadway to the fabled North Beach intersection where the topless tourist bars, the jazz and coffeehouse row that spawned the hippies' beatnik ancestors, and North America's largest Chinatown all met.

The taxi turned onto Grant Street, Chinatown's main artery, and continued half a dozen blocks up the darkened thoroughfare until it passed beneath the huge ornamental gate that was the symbolic center of Chinatown. A fast right turn and then a left, and the cab halted before a labyrinth of narrow alleyways that hugged the side of a steep hillside.

The passengers got out. There was a distinguished older Chinese with silver-gray hair and a mustache. He wore a black homburg and a dark trenchcoat to keep out the chill. The other man was taller and younger, but he paced nervously alongside the taxi with mincing steps. He clutched an attaché case with desperate intensity and peered around into the fog, his dark eyes popping froglike behind thick, round, wire-rimmed glasses. There was something almost comical about his agitation in the murky street as his lips slid fidgeting around a mousy, protruding set of buckteeth.

The cab pulled away and the suave older man led the way toward an impressive shop secured behind a grille of iron bars. And then the waiting attackers came out of the nearby alleyways. . . .

There were five of the shadowy figures, two with submachine guns and the others holding pistols. The orders came hissing out in a flat California accent, "Okay, Shu Lin. You and your flunky hold it right there. Just hand over the antique jade stuff you brought over from Hong Kong and we won't have to hurt you."

The older man nodded and the tall, popeyed young man stepped forward, trembling as he held out the attaché case. One of the robbers advanced and snatched it out of his hand. The rest of the gunmen crowded around as their leader snapped open the case to make sure the loot was really there.

The silly-looking young Oriental and his employer bowed their heads away, as if in shame at losing their valuable shipment so easily.

And then a flash of hellfire flared white-hot through the murky fog, blinding the five gunmen!

It was a magnesium strip, boobytrapped to go off if the attaché case was opened without first pressing a hidden switch. And as the gunmen instinctively pressed their hands to their temporarily useless eyes, the young man who had been holding the briefcase made a spectacular, catlike dive to the sidewalk and rolled over twice, crashing into the legs of the knot of robbers like a human battering ram.

The gunmen went down in a clump of ragdoll bodies, most of them dropping their weapons in a reflex attempt to break the sudden fall. They were all youthful Chinese, with slender but hard-muscled bodies and tough, grim faces.

The first gunman to blink back his hurt irises into some semblance of vision saw a tall shape kneeling over him. He reached out to find his automatic rifle but a small, white missile was suddenly hurtling toward his head with a kind of "phoot" sound. It was hard and sharp, a little rock that slashed into his cheek and drew blood.

The supposed "flunky" had spit out his false set of buckteeth at the Chinese gangster. And now he whipped off his absurdly thick eyeglasses, clutched them in his fist like a knife and stabbed down. The wire sidebar was like a razor as the blow buried the eyeglasses deep into the punk's neck and he passed out with a gurgling cry.

The other four gunmen were starting to scramble to their feet again and the young bodyguard sprang up. He tossed back his head and his long, glossy, black hair leaped away from its old-fashioned center part to fall down below his ears in a mod, casual style.

Without the simple but effective disguise of bottle eyeglasses and protruding false teeth, the bodyguard looked totally different. His face, in fact, was remarkably memorable. The features were basically Chinese, except for the nose being slightly sharper and the eyes somewhat less slanted than the norm. But his complexion was a near-translucent marbled gold, light enough to be an unmistakable sign of Eurasian mixed parentage.

Without the mincing walk and hunched carriage he had adopted, it could now be seen that he was much taller and broader-shouldered than the average Oriental, perhaps a shade over six feet. He took a moment to stretch, in luxuriant relief from the cramped posture of his disguise, and the breadth of his chest almost tore through the cheap cotton fabric of the plain white shirt he had adopted for his role. He snatched up to loosen the stringy dark necktie around his throat, and then on second thought he ripped the tie apart and flipped it away from him with an easy tug of his fingers.

The first of the gunmen to recover was scrambling to his feet. It was the leader who had demanded the attaché case. The Eurasian bodyguard's leg snaked out like a writhing fire hose under full pressure. The heel of his heavy businessman's oxford crashed into the goon's chin and he toppled over onto another arising hoodlum.

The bodyguard heard the scrape of metal on the concrete sidewalk behind him. He whirled about in a blur of incredible speed. His arm zoomed out like a scythe before him and the flat of his palm slammed over an assailant's ear an instant before the pistol the crook was holding went off and the bullet buzzed harmlessly into the fog. Blood fountained from the ruptured eardrum as the bodyguard pulled his hand away. The hoodlum rolled over, moaning agonizedly.

One of the two remaining yet-unscathed hoodlums scrambled backwards on his knees, ignoring the death-dealing automatic rifle beside him because of his panic. He pointed a trembling finger at the bodyguard and yelled, "Goddamn, it's Tommy Lee. I'm getting out of here." He leaped up and darted off into the fog as the bodyguard made no attempt to stop him.

The other unharmed gangster scurried off after his partner. Swiftly, the bodyguard scooped up all the weapons from the sidewalk and walked off, without a backward glance at his moaning fallen assailants.

He moved toward the jade shop, pausing en route to pick up under one arm the small pile of overseas luggage which had been unloaded from the airport taxi. The barred grill had been unlocked and slid slightly aside. The bodyguard tapped lightly at the door four times with the tip of a shoe.

In a moment, the older Chinese opened the door to the darkened showroom. The two men moved away from the re-locked door and passed through an ornate brocaded curtain to a large, comfortable workroom at the rear of the shop. There the older man spread out his expensive trenchcoat on a large table. He unzipped the fleeced winter lining and began to empty the rows of hidden zippered pockets on the inside of the lining.

Ancient jade treasures from mainland China began to appear atop the soft fabric as the shopowner's careful hands removed the pieces from the hidden pouches. There were rings and necklaces of silver or gold surrounding the rich green stones as well as charming statuettes carved painstakingly from single large pieces of jade.

"You proved worthy of your seemingly exorbitant fee after all, Tommy," said the shopowner. "That was a remarkable display of the martial arts against armed men out there."

Tommy Lee grinned as he set down his burden of luggage and guns. "Shame on you, Shu Lin," he told the debonaire jade importer who had hired him. "You know that we agreed if there was any trouble at this end you would go directly into the shop and call the police. How do you expect to live to a wise old age if you take such unnecessary risks?"

Shu Lin responded, "A long life is meaningless without the spice of adventure, my son. And adventure always entails some risk."

"Okay, I'm glad you enjoyed the fight," said Tommy. "But how about calling the police? There's no reason to be shy on pressing charges against these scum, just because they are of our people."

The jade merchant nodded. "As soon as I saw you had won the struggle, I came inside with our valuable goods and pressed the alarm button that goes to district police headquarters. The officers should be here shortly."

"Fine, maybe they'll still be able to catch some of that garbage I left outside. My own first responsibility is to make sure you get your goods locked securely in your office safe."

The merchant continued taking jade pieces out of the hidden coat-liner pockets. "It is sad how in recent years some young Chinese have become so lawless. Not only here in San Francisco Chinatown but in all our settlements around the world there are violent gangs of Chinese Youth. Such things did not exist in my day."

"Please, let's not get sanctimonious about young Chinese," laughed Tommy Lee. "When you were growing up here, the Tong Wars and the killings done by ferocious hatchet men had the white citizens shaking in their boots.

If things got temporarily quieter around Chinatown for thirty years or so, it's not because the Chinese got namby-pamby suddenly. It's just that suddenly the society opened up a lot more legal opportunities and that used up a lot of energy from the oriental minorities. Anyway, most Chinese-Americans now were born here rather than the old country and you see more of the traditional melting-pot effect. The old country rules seem less meaningful to a kid who grows up in a Chinatown that's really a slum, no matter how quaint a slum it looks like to tourists. Non-whites everywhere in the world are demanding more equal opportunity. Why should Chinatown be different from the black ghettos of the Third World nations?"

"The fact remains, Tommy Lee, that you yourself are in the classic tradition of the Chinese fighting man. As I observed only a few minutes ago, you are the perfect contemporary model of the tong assassin, a hatchet man of today." Shu Lin had flung open a hinged painting that hid his thick wall safe and was dialing open the combination.

"I'm no assassin," said Tommy good-humoredly. "I'm a private detective with licensed branch offices in eleven cities from New York to Bangkok. That's big business, not a freelance hatchet man racket. I'm going to bill you by computer for escorting your shipment safely from Hong Kong. What kind of hatchet man ever did that?"

The jade merchant didn't answer while he placed his valuable new shipment inside the safe and slammed the steel door shut. Then he said slowly, "All I can tell you is that ten or twenty years ago I would not have felt it was necessary to hire an assassin—forgive me, a licensed private detective—to protect my life and goods from young Chinese boys in my home city. Something very dangerous, whether it's new or simply a return to the more explosive side of the Chinese nature, is happening. True, your own respected father Chan Hoy Lee was quite a pirate in his younger days before he attained enough wealth to become a legitimate businessman. And I feel we of the tongs may have great need of trustworthy master assassins like you, no matter what you call yourself, in perilous days soon to come."

"I hope you're wrong, honored Shu Lin," said Tommy Lee. But both men knew that the depredations of heavily armed Chinese youth gangs in San Francisco had been getting increasingly wilder and more dangerous.

CHAPTER TWO

By the time Tommy Lee awoke late next morning, it was as if the dense fog of yesterday had never existed. A bright, cheerful sun had chewed up last night's remaining fog tendrils and now San Francisco was bathed in its usual soft, poetic beauty.

Tommy could see most of the city, as well as out into the bay, from the floor-to-ceiling glass walls of his corner apartment in a spectacular new high-rise atop a hill near the waterfront. This was more his home than anyplace else in the world, although he was continuously on the go as president and founder of East-West Investigations, a unique and highly successful private security agency with offices in Hong Kong, Saigon, Manila, Bangkok, Singapore, Tokyo, Taiwan, Seoul, San Francisco, Vancouver, and New York.

Although barely thirty, Tommy Lee's annual personal income was well over $100,000 and he was no slouch at indulging his luxurious tastes in clothes, housing, cars, and his sex life. The secret of the skyrocketing success of East-West Investigations was that Tommy was perfectly at home at every level of society throughout the Orient and in every major Chinatown district of the West.

The Far East and its Chinatown annexes had long been recognized as world hotbeds of bizarre intrigue. Now with the newly booming manufacturing economy of Asia, there were ever-growing needs for secure dealings between giant business corporations of Asia and the Western nations.

That was where Tommy Lee fit in. Despite his youth, he had been a brilliantly successful undercover agent since he was drafted into the U.S. Army at the age of nineteen.

He was then a hot-blooded young man facing the classic choice of the military or jail, after the bigoted father of Tommy's seventeen-year-old white girlfriend bullied her into telling the police a rape story.

When the Pentagon computers got a look at his Eurasian background—especially his fluency in every major Asiatic language and dialect—they must have lit up and flashed jackpot! Tommy was snapped up by the Army Counter-Intelligence Corps, trained as a field agent and shipped right to Vietnam where U.S. involvement was still holding the gallant illusions of the JFK Green Beret days.

He soon disappointed his right-wing superiors with his "political unreliability" as democratic opponents of U.S.-sponsored dictatorships had an unfailing ability to slip through his fingers. But once the brass tried him out as an undercover investigator of Vietnamese corruption, he became an intensely deadly foe of the callous criminal gangs making a fortune by hijacking U.S. medical supplies or refugee relief food.

Word of Tommy's growing reputation soon leaked to other U.S. Intelligence services. Repeatedly, political muscle was used to borrow Tommy's services for tough cases throughout Asia by the Army Criminal Investigation Division, Navy or Air Force Intelligence, or the National Security Agency. But the Department of Defense agencies jealously drew the line at lending him out to the CIA. Then when Tommy's two-year military obligation was up and he laughed off pleadings to re-enlist, the Pentagon was so determined to keep him away from any possible CIA clutches that they made him an offer he couldn't refuse.

At the age of twenty-two Tommy Lee had a four-year contract for $3000 a month and practically unlimited expenses as an agent of the Defense Intelligence Agency, on call throughout Asia for all the military intelligence divisions. By the time this lucrative and adventuresome hitch was over, Tommy was operating largely beyond the realm of lower-level criminals and working on cases of industrial supply-line security all through our allied territories of the Far East. He dealt with many of Asia's most influential men and the ultimate natural result was East-West Investigations and its quick success as a much-needed new service for the booming industrial trade between the Orient and the Occident.

On waking this morning, Tommy stumbled to the shower and rinsed the top layers of jet lag from his body. He put on a thick terrycloth robe and padded to his kitchen to make some richly aromatic coffee on a futuristic imported Swiss brewer.

He carried the cup of coffee around the majestic apartment, sipping at it as he shaved, combed, and got dressed. He chose a dark blue suit with a vest that looked as if it were from one of Paris or London's top tailors, but in fact came from Hong Kong at half the price.

Tommy Lee's spectacular heritage fit him perfectly for the unique detective he had become. His father was one of the typical Chinese breed of highrolling wheeler-dealers, alternately wealthy or down to the family's last dollars as he hopscotched around Asia and the West's Chinatowns, setting up and selling one business after another. His mother was a beautiful and hot-blooded White Russian refugee whose Czarist cossack officer family fled Communism to Hong Kong in the 1930s.

Both families at first disowned the mixed marriage of Chan Hoy and Verushka Lee, yet the pair remained together for some forty stormy but loving years. Only a heart attack finally sidelined the senior Lee and he was in semi-retirement at the rural Hawaiian inn he and his wife owned. Besides Tommy, the marriage produced an older sister who was a doctor at Singapore's largest hospital and a younger brother who flew for Taiwan Airlines.

Tommy Lee was born in San Francisco during World War II. His father got the family out of Asia one jump ahead of the Japanese blitzkreig and then offered his services to the OSS as a spy. Chan Hoy became one of America's most valuable secret agents in the Far East and while he was recklessly risking his life for a cause he believed in, he didn't ignore the opportunity to smuggle jewels and gold home from each mission.

With the war won, Chan Hoy Lee took his family and

an impressive grubstake back to the Far East and made an expanding success in business as the region's economy started to take off. Tommy spent the bulk of his adolescence in Hong Kong, but also traveled widely with his parents throughout Asia at an age when he was young enough to pick up languages almost automatically.

Constantly being a mixed-blood newcomer in school among suspicious teenagers, Tommy naturally had to fight off a lot of bullies. He began studying the martial arts as a child, ranking as an expert in Hong Kong's freestyle street-fighting kung fu and also during his travels picking up the most valuable elements of karate, aikido, and judo. As it turned out eventually, Tommy often couldn't carry a gun during his military undercover assignments. But that didn't matter, because his martial arts skills enabled him to disarm any single opponent bare-handed and then use the confiscated weapon on any other armed opponents.

Tommy checked himself in the mirror before he left for his local office. He wasn't in any special rush to get to the desk; if there was some emergency business, the East-West staff knew they could reach him at the apartment this morning. Attired in his usual mod style, as he was today, Tommy made a striking figure, especially with his distinctive light gold skin color. Yet the complexion did not give him away when he needed to disguise himself as an ordinary Chinese. A sunlamp or a few hours at the beach were enough to darken his skin to the normal Chinese hue.

Down in front of his luxurious high-rise, Tommy chatted with the doorman about San Francisco goings-on during the three weeks he'd been away in the Orient. A garage attendant zoomed up from the basement with Tommy's gleaming white Jaguar XKE and the detective took off.

East-West Investigations had its world headquarters here in an architectural showpiece skyscraper between Chinatown and the financial district of San Francisco. In decorative style, the building had a strong Oriental feeling. And fittingly enough, it was a center for offices that served the complex Asia-U.S. trade network and its construction had been financed by an international real estate consortium.

Tommy parked his Jaguar in the reserved basement slot and rode up to the 41st floor in an elevator that looked like a Japanese teahouse. The doors to his suite of offices had the brass-lettered East-West Investigations blocked out in six Oriental languages as well as English.

The EWI reception area was done in futuristic plastic furniture from Japan. Behind the desk was a beautiful young Chinese girl with luscious breast mounds looming un-brassiered behind a silk bodyshirt with the Rolling Stones tongue symbol done in delicate beadwork.

"Hi, Cuz," she said cheerfully. "How's it hanging? You like my shirt? It's the latest thing."

Her name was Lotus Fong and she was a second cousin of Tommy's. In the strict Chinese codes of extended family loyalty, sex between second cousins would be as unthinkably incestuous as getting it on with one's mother. Fortunately, Tommy and Lotus had been raised together through much of their childhood and thought of each other in exclusively brother-sister terms.

They each led separately fulfilling sex lives and their continual erotic teasing of each other was a game, a displaying of an unusual relationship between two lusty young people. They particularly enjoyed blowing the minds of outsiders with their raunchy carryings-on but found it funny even when by themselves.

"That tongue makes you look like a groupie with no tits," said Tommy.

Involuntarily, Lotus glanced down at her impressively bobbing cleavage. "What the hell do you mean, no tits?" she grumbled.

Tommy reached over the desk and squeezed one breast gently, appreciating the sensory impact of the lovely soft womanliness without getting aroused by it. "Oh yeah, there they are," he said. "I guess what you have to do is suck in your tummy to make them stick out more."

Lotus squirmed out of his grasp, stuck out her tongue at him and grabbed a pile of papers on the desk. Swiftly she rolled the papers into a cylinder and tried to swat at Tommy's balls but he stepped back out of range in plenty of time.

"A shitty way to welcome back your boss, Ms. Fong," he said. "Young Chinese women of today have no respect."

"Yes sir, I hear that from my parents all the time, and from Grandpa Harvey in the office too." Harvey Fong somehow managed to be Tommy's uncle and Lotus's grandfather simultaneously. A dapper, well-fed man in his late fifties, he was EWI's administrative director, a master of accounting and computerization. Tommy had a score of relatives among the staff of one hundred and fifty spread among EWI's eleven branch offices.

It was the Chinese way and made a lot of sense in terms of ensuring a higher sense of loyalty throughout a far-flung business operation. In most matters, although Tommy was half white he thought of himself as an Oriental with an unusually good understanding of caucasian viewpoints. This was natural enough, since he had grown up mainly in the Far East and among his father's big family and clan of associates rather than his Russian mother's struggling circle of anti-red exiles.

"Okay, Lotus, any important business waiting for me?" he asked. They both knew it was now business time and enough kidding around had gone down for this session.

"No red alerts. You'll find the paperwork on all current reports at your desk in the in-box, arranged in order of importance."

"Fine."

"The only other thing is a Miss Delmonico who's been calling for you. She's asked for a full security deployment at some kind of meeting or party tomorrow night. But she insists that you take personal charge of the job if you're in town and I said we expected you in the office this afternoon."

"A lady named Delmonico? I don't know her."

"Then you've got a treat in store, Cuz. I hate to admit it, but she's a real gorgeous broad. Lots of wavy black hair, big hazel eyes, legs that don't quit. Just the kind of client you like to have around."

"In that case, get her on the phone for me after I've had half an hour with the in-box and we'll help reassure her that EWI can take care of her problems."

CHAPTER THREE

"I thought I'd just come over rather than explain what we need on the phone," said Lisa Delmonico. "Communication is so much better in person, don't you think?"

"Oh, I couldn't agree more," said Tommy. He stood up smoothly and, after shaking hands with the lady through her butter-soft kidskin glove, he ushered her into a comfortable slingback leather chair in front of his impressive oaken desk.

Tommy's private office was very Northern California, all rich woods and leather in distinctive customized shapes. Delicate Chinese ink drawings shared wall space with old Fillmore rock concert posters, yet the entire multi-cultural melange blended comfortably into a hip and comfortable whole.

He certainly had no objections to the Delmonico woman popping in on him. She was as stunning as Cousin Lotus had promised and even more exciting than another non-lesbian woman would have realized.

Lisa Delmonico was groomed and dressed impeccably, in the style of a high society deb out for a lunch date. She wore a floppy white felt hat that dramatically set off the boldly high cheekbones of her exotic face. A fur-trimmed suede coat was casually draped over her shoulders and beneath it she wore a dark red tailored suit with over-the-knee skirt that revealed lovely legs in the sheerest of hosiery. Her delicate ankles crossed over glistening glove-textured pumps with clunky medium platform heels.

But the most dominant impression about her was of utter poise, cool sophistication overlying an animal intensity that wasn't cold at all. Her entire manner was challengingly self-confident. Without losing her femininity, she gave off a kind of bold forcefulness, a sense of dynamic action, that would be found in few women.

Tommy sensed immediately that his newest client was a rare type of human being and he had every intention of trying to put their dealings beyond the business level if he could.

"We have a very competent staff here at the San Francisco office, Miss Delmonico. I'm sure they could have handled all your security problems without my direct supervision," he said. "But of course I'm pleased that my business brought me back to town in time to get personally involved."

"It's not that we don't have confidence in your local associates, Mr. Lee. But there are extremely high stakes involved in the meeting my father is holding here tomorrow. We want the very best protection available and expense is no object."

"Please tell me all about it," said Tommy. "Exactly what is it that you think your business meeting needs protecting against?"

Lisa crossed her legs prettily and said, "You see, my father has gotten a direct threat of extortion against the meeting from some sort of Chinatown gang. The letter said we'd have to pay $200,000 or the meeting would be turned into a bloodbath."

Tommy sighed, "Extortion isn't exactly new in Chinatown. But I've never heard of anything quite so blatant from our gangs. It seems there really is an unprecedented climate of violence building among Chinese criminals. I want to see the extortion letter. What's the name of the gang that sent it?"

"Oh dear, I'm afraid my father has the letter and he won't be in town till late tomorrow," she said. "I don't think there was any signature to the threat."

"That's too bad, we need some information in order to counterattack." Tommy drummed his fingers on the desk. "But since we're on the defensive, fill me in about the meeting I'm guarding."

"The actual business being discussed is something I

must keep secret, you understand. My father is Bartlett Delmonico, the international financier, and he's bringing together about a dozen important associates to put together a very complicated deal that could involve worldwide control of a valuable commodity. I'm the advanceman." She smiled to herself at the term. "I do a lot of confidential work for Daddy, I'm sort of his de facto administrative assistant."

"You'll have to forgive me, but I've never heard of Bartlett Delmonico," Tommy said.

"That's not surprising. For a wealthy man, Daddy has been unusually successful at not making waves and keeping out of the news. Our official residence is Bermuda, for tax reasons. Not that we stay very long in any place. And you'll find Daddy listed in Dun & Bradstreet's credit directory with the top rating."

"Where is this meeting exactly?"

"We rented a mansion in Pacific Heights for three days. It's a furnished place you can get on short-term lease. By the way, my father has his own personal security staff and so do most of the other people coming to the conference. Because of the confidential nature of the meeting, we don't want any of your men inside the mansion. Our own people will be taking care of that."

"Oh? Then why exactly are you seeking out a Chinese-American detective agency? What do you want us to do?"

"Well, naturally we expect you to use your Chinatown contacts to try and get a trace on the extortion gang, even though I realize we haven't given you hardly anything to go on. Also, we'd want you to station as many reliable men as you can get in the street around the mansion—as our outer ring of defense. We're hoping that your knowledge of Chinatown would enable you to spot a threat before our people could and deal with it at the safest distance from the conference room."

"Understood. I can field about fifteen top men, cover the neighboring rooftops and all that. You know, of course, you could always have paid the $200,000 demand."

"Even for millionaires like Daddy and his friends, $200,000 cash isn't exactly spare change. Not that we've ruled out the idea completely, but we'd rather spend money to protect ourselves than give in to extortion. Also, we're interested in finding out exactly how word of our meeting leaked out so it doesn't happen again and foul up the entire deal. Putting you on the case would seem to be the best way to go about that."

"I'll need to have a look at the house layout so I can start making my deployment plans," said Tommy. "Can you show me around?"

"Of course, I'm at your disposal."

Tommy grinned. "Then let's do it after a late lunch, Miss Delmonico. I know a place where we can get the best Ramos Gin Fizz in the Bay Area."

"I'd be delighted, Mr. Lee."

"Would you just wait for me in the reception lobby for a minute? I've got to make one phone call on a confidential matter."

"Certainly, I'd like to powder my nose anyway."

As soon as Lisa left the room, Tommy riffled through his rolodex file and got the number of a private detective in Miami who handed EWI business in the area. "Get me a quick rundown on a moneyman named Bartlett Delmonico who's supposed to be based out of Bermuda and have a daughter named Lisa," requested Tommy. "I'll phone you back later in the day."

By the end of a long, enjoyable lunch, Miss Delmonico and Mr. Lee had been dropped in favor of Lisa and Tommy. Now the handsome young pair was pulling up in Tommy's white Jaguar before the Pacific Heights mansion where the international business meeting was to take place.

Tommy noted approvingly that the big victorian house was surrounded by a solid whitewashed stucco wall with a wide ironwork gate at the center. Right now the gate was open and Tommy drove right into the small courtyard. Lisa hopped out and moved gracefully to the front door, with Tommy following.

"A lot of Daddy's staff is here already," she said. "The security people are checking out the house and Daddy's electronics consultant is going over the place for bugs. And of course the kitchen crew and clean-up girls are stocking up. The guests will be staying over for the entire conference once they arrive."

In answer to the doorbell's ring, they were let in by a chunky and rather broken-faced guardian whose expensive suit didn't make him look any less like a classic street ruffian.

"Bill, this is Mr. Lee. His detective agency will be patrolling the street for us and I'm going to show him the inside layout."

The toughie nodded and ambled away. Tommy whispered quizzically to Lisa, "For a business tycoon, your father has got a real hood type cat working as his bodyguard."

Lisa giggled, "What would you expect, some rabbity little man who couldn't scare his own shadow? Naturally Daddy is looking for toughness in his security force."

She guided him through the gracious two-story house. The place was furnished in quiet good taste and there was nothing unusual about it. Tommy approved the choice of conference room, a den in the middle of the house with no windows. Through the upstairs windows he could see a couple of tall neighboring apartment buildings that had vantage points for snipers and he made a note to stake out the roofs and lobbies.

Then a booming voice from the front hall was calling out, "Lisa, Lisa."

Lisa raised her voice to answer immediately, "Here, Daddy, I'm in back with Mr. Lee."

An imposing figure approached to greet them. Bartlett Delmonico was a tall, powerfully built man with a craggy Mediterranean face and glossy black hair whose only concession to middle age was a slight retreat back from the forehead. His only immediately recognizable resemblance to his daughter was in the snapping intensity of their dark brown eyes.

"Tommy Lee, so my daughter did manage to get through to you," he said. "I'm delighted. My contacts said you're absolutely the best man for surveillance work having anything to do with Chinatown."

"Did you have a nice flight in the Learjet, Daddy?" Lisa hurried to give him a fast hug and a kiss on the mouth.

"Smooth all the way, honey. Mr. Lee, have you got a line on these extortionists yet?"

"I'm afraid not. I only got started on your problem a few hours ago. I was hoping you'd have the extortion note with you."

"Damn, I don't. I left it home. Didn't realize the paper would be important, which I suppose now was pretty careless of me. Anyway, it was just a short, unsigned note of a few sentences."

"How were you supposed to make contact to pay the $200,000?"

"They ordered me to have a messenger with the money waiting by a certain phone booth at Fisherman's Wharf and they'd give him instructions from there. Of course, I didn't do it, for reasons I imagine Lisa explained to you."

"It's too bad I wasn't available in town earlier," said Tommy. "It would have been a good idea to send a fake messenger to the rendezvous and see if we could flush anything out."

"You're right, of course. I guess this sort of thing simply isn't the kind of intrigue I'm used to in the business world," said Delmonico. "Well, if you two will excuse me I want to check on how the preparations are coming and then relax for a while after the flight. Lisa, I'll see you when you're done with Mr. Lee."

He marched off, with Bill the tough-looking bodyguard coming up to escort him. Lisa turned to Tommy and said casually, "Well, is that all for now? Have you seen enough?"

Tommy looked at the beautiful girl carefully. He was just starting to feel like his usual cocky, happy-go-lucky self again after the strain and disorientation of the long flight from Hong Kong yesterday and the fierce fight in the fog that followed.

"I'd like to have one more look at a bedroom upstairs," he said. "Something's been nagging at the back of my mind for the last few minutes and I just got a hold on it. There was a kind of reflection from one of the apartment buildings across the street that just might be a telescope mounted on a tripod."

"Well, let's have a look."

"You don't need to go with me if you have to talk to your father.... On second thought, it *would* be better if we both went upstairs. If somebody is watching us through a scope, I don't want him to realize I'm up there trying to spot him."

"Come on," said Lisa. "You're making me feel like a real Mata Hari."

Tommy led the way to one of the more comfortable and pretty bedrooms he had noticed on his previous tour upstairs. He stood by the window with his arm around Lisa's shoulders, casually looking out at the street.

"I thought I spotted something before on the third floor from the top," he said. "Over toward the left corner."

"I don't see any unusual reflection spot now," Lisa said thoughtfully.

"Neither do I," Tommy admitted. "Maybe it was the angle of vision. I wasn't looking directly out the window when I noticed the flare."

He turned Lisa around so she was facing him and looked over her head at a sideward angle. "Nothing up there now," he said. "Either I was wrong or they moved the scope. Just have your boys keep an eye on those windows every once in a while."

But now, of course, Lisa was standing close against him and as he looked down into her eyes it was just a smooth move to pull her against him and kiss her. Lisa's lips were as elegantly exciting as anything he could have expected.

Her soft, slender arms moved around him and the kiss grew more passionate. There were definite sparks flying between the pair by the time they moved their mouths apart.

Lisa said, "I realized this would happen sooner or later. So it might as well happen now." Casually, she stepped back and started taking off her jacket. "I think it might be a good idea if you locked the door," she suggested.

CHAPTER FOUR

He took her atop the brocaded bedspread, their clothing tossed casually along the floor nearby.

Lisa Delmonico, from the first, was an active partner in the transaction of sex. Despite her aloof, high-society bearing the passive role was not for her.

She clung to Tommy, her hands working diligently as she told him in no over-subtle terms exactly what she required him to do to her. Her teeth were taking little nips at his shoulders.

Tommy had experienced a wider variety of the world's women than most males, from the shy flower-maidens of Thailand to the lusty wenches of Sweden. But he knew a beautiful female as overpoweringly passionate as Lisa was a rare treasure indeed.

As for Tommy, he had grown up with the rich tradition of classic Chinese lovemaking in which one of the main goals of each partner is to bring the other to intense orgasm without coming oneself. This is supposed to be done by a wild abandon in lovemaking performed while consciously holding back one's own climax.

As a modern man, Tommy Lee was highly dubious about the pseudo-scientific medical theories behind the Chinese erotic doctrine of withholding sperm during the climax of sexual intercourse. This was supposed to retain the potency of the seed, or the love juices in the case of the woman, inside one's own body and thus produce long-lasting youthfulness and health.

Still, Tommy liked the pleasurable side-effects of withholding his climax for the longest possible time and this was his basic style of lovemaking, coupled with a tiger-like abandonment that kept his sensations at fever pitch and didn't distress his lovers either.

Lisa seemed to have arrived at her own version of this ancient Chinese art naturally. She threw herself into sex like a berserk Venus, yet it was clear that her piledriving vaginal churnings were the result of a consciously willed plunge into erotic thrills, not a desire that had swept over her uncontrollably.

Though Tommy was not really used to getting back so much of his own treatment on such short acquaintance, his wide practice enabled him to hang in there far longer than most Western males could have under this strong stimulus.

In fact, his wracking shudders at just about the point of coming were seemingly what set off Lisa's own tremendous climax. The lovely girl's sensuously slender body nearly exploded beneath him. In her final spasm she arched her back in a fierce bow that lifted his entire body off the bed.

When they were both lying sprawled and spent across the bed, Lisa said, "You've struck a blow against blind prejudice. Now I know another racial myth isn't true."

Tommy laughed. This was a familiar topic to him. "You mean the myth that all Oriental men have small penises?" he said.

"That's right. And now I believe that the lie was spread by men of other races, out of jealousy."

To Tommy's astonishment, she was already on her feet again and getting dressed. Lisa's powers of self-control and recovery were truly astonishing.

She told him, "Take your time, darling. I want to go find out what Daddy needs me for." She blew him a kiss and started to leave the room.

"I'll be back with my men tomorrow afternoon to set up the cordon," Tommy said. "Meantime, I'll have our Chinatown gang contacts checked out to see if we can get a line on who's trying to muscle your father."

"That's wonderful, Tommy. I know you'll do your best."

He dressed unhurriedly and left the sprawling house,

taking note of all the bustling preparations going on inside. Something of large scale was obviously to be decided at this conference.

Driving back to the office in his XKE, he got his Miami affiliate on the car phone for a report on the Delmonico family.

"Yeah, there's a Delmonico family in Bermuda, Tommy," said the Florida detective. "Father and daughter pretty well fit the description you gave me. The old man is in money and travels a lot. They apparently haven't been home for about three weeks. One thing funny, the daughter is known around here as Elizabeth. But the names are close enough so that I suppose she could be called by both. Anyway, I've got some photos and a written rundown that I'm putting into the mail air special delivery."

"Thanks," said Tommy. "At least I know they check out as legit."

The next day as late afternoon shadows mellowed into a perfect San Francisco sunset, Tommy Lee was parked inside a delivery truck waiting thirty yards away from the conference mansion.

This truck was Tommy's command post for a crack EWI team of sixteen men stationed all around the Pacific Heights mansion. He was in touch with all of them by walkie-talkie radio and could see the street perfectly through a strip of one-way mirror that bordered both sides of the truck van. Lettering on the side of the truck said it came from Mandarin Glass Corp., so the decorative border of mirror didn't seem out of place.

The van was also studded with gunports that unlatched only from the inside, as well as being armored throughout with bulletproof metal.

Tommy scanned the street with binoculars through the one-way mirror. There were two EWI operatives in the truck with him. Harry Chow, the electronics man, had just completed a radio call circuit of all the other detectives hidden on rooftops and in alleyways around the house. Joe Loosan, the driver, was waiting in the van with a shotgun cradled across his lap.

"All set, chief," said Chow. "Everybody's in place with their communications in working order."

Tommy looked at the gold digital watch on his wrist. According to the timetable he had been given by Lisa earlier in the day, the conference participants should be arriving momentarily now. They would be coming in limousines from their separately chartered jets at the airport. From what he had been told about the extortion note, Tommy didn't expect any violent action against the conference until all parties were assembled.

A long black Cadillac with liveried chauffeur pulled up before the mansion. Tommy trained the binoculars on the rear license plate and verified that the numbers tallied with an approved limo license on the list he'd been given.

The Caddy had stopped by a brown sedan parked right alongside the driveway to the gate. This was a main guardpost manned by Delmonico's own people, those surprisingly street-tough types on his personal security staff. They had a walkie-talkie for communication with Tommy in the van too.

The limousine driver and occupants must have passed inspection by the armed guards parked alongside the gate. They passed in through the driveway and after disembarking in the courtyard the lone driver came out again and took off.

In the next forty minutes, the process was repeated three times with small groups of men in limousines whose license plates tallied with the official list. All the conference attendees were safely inside now and Tommy settled down for a long night of surveillance.

This was one of the most frustrating parts of real detective work. Hour after hour of waiting on the alert, with the simple problems of food and excretion gradually taking on major importance. At least Tommy had a coffeemaker, refrigerator and toilet compartment in the van, which was more than the others standing out in the dusk could rely on.

It was another two hours and into full evening before anything else happened.

A food supply truck marked from Atlas Vending

pulled up by the gate. Tommy swiftly rechecked his list. Atlas Vending was on the roster of prearranged suppliers to the conference, but they weren't due to make a delivery until tomorrow afternoon.

The truck was about the same size as Tommy's communications van and the driver looked Chinese. But of course there were Chinese working at all sorts of jobs throughout San Francisco, so this didn't mean anything in itself.

Tommy observed closely as one of Delmonico's private guards poked his head out of their car window to query the delivery driver. All his EWI staff's efforts during the previous night had brought no gang information leaks about a threat against any conference and Tommy knew anything could happen.

Then Harry Chow snatched the binoculars out of Tommy's hands and focused on the delivery driver. "I know that guy," he said excitedly. "It's Ben Moo Ling, a punk who used to be in the Young Swordsmen. See the way his left arm is kind of bent? He messed it up in a motorcycle spill two years ago."

Instantly, Tommy grabbed the radio microphone, pressed the transmission button and sent out a warning to the gate guards. Their brown car doors flipped open and the guards began to leap out with their pistols drawn.

But suddenly the Atlas Vending truck sign proved to be only a cardboard covering over a panel cut out in the side of the rear van. Two submachine gun snouts poked through the paper and began spraying a rain of death bullets into Delmonico's men.

In a flash the guards were out of action and the fake vending truck was speeding away.

Joe Loosan was already darting behind the steering wheel of Tommy's truck. "Go get them," Tommy shouted in command.

The EWI truck, powered by a big engine originally meant for a full trailer rig, catapulted away from the curb in a screech of tires. Tommy snatched his shotgun off the rack near the ceiling and pushed it through an appropriate gunport beneath the one-way mirror.

These guys with their illegal automatic rifles obviously meant business, thought Tommy as he waited for Joe to bring them within range. Going right up to the front gate like that meant this gang, whoever they were, was willing to make an all-out direct assault on the conference despite the hair-raising risk to their own lives. But kamikaze tactics were not the Chinese style and Tommy couldn't understand what volatile new formula was at work here.

The two fake delivery trucks careened through the steep, narrow streets around Pacific Heights at lurching speed. Joe was a brilliant driver and mechanic, so in a few moments they were close enough for Tommy to start pumping out shots at the escaping truck's tires.

But the angle of fire from the gunports was wrong. The other truck's tires were largely hidden behind metal plates and he couldn't get off a clear shot.

Tommy returned the shotgun to the rack and shouted to the driver, "Joe, see if you can get alongside the other truck for just a few seconds. Like within nudging distance."

The driver nodded and floored the gas pedal. The lumbering box of the EWI truck shot forward and closed on the fleeing vehicle. A burst of automatic fire came from the gang's machine guns, bouncing harmlessly off the bulletproof glass and metal. Joe didn't even bother to duck behind the wheel.

Tommy made sure his .44 magnum Smith & Wesson revolver was snug in the shoulder holster and then he pushed open one of the van's rear doors, propping it into the full open position. He reached up for the roof of the truck and in one easy motion hauled his body up onto the flat metal bed and rolled himself into the center.

He sprawled out flat but raised his head to check the range. Joe had already barreled up nearly alongside the gang truck and showed no sign of falling behind. Good enough!

Tommy got into a crouch and easily sprang across the two narrow feet of space that separated the two trucks. He landed flat, taking the impact on his outspread palms and clinging tight to the roof to keep from being buffeted off by the windstream.

He waited there just long enough to re-establish his equilibrium and then crawled to the front of the truck. Grasping tightly to the rubber stripping around the windshield with one hand, he unholstered his revolver with the other and leaned down over the windshield of the speeding vehicle.

He gave an upside-down grin to the two figures inside the truck cab and tapped at the glass with his gunbarrel to get their attention.

The young Chinese seated beside the driver started raising his submachine gun toward Tommy's face after a frozen moment of shock. Tommy pulled the trigger. The impact of the big magnum cartridge splintered most of the windshield and the gunman was slammed back into his seat with blood gushing out of his chest.

The driver didn't stop and surrender as Tommy had planned. Instead, he fishtailed the steering wheel and crushed down on the brake in order to dislodge Tommy from the roof.

There was no way Tommy could hold on. Tossing the gun away from him, he tucked himself into a ball and somersaulted as far from the truck as he could get. Out of the corner of his eye he could see an angle of sidewalk and wall coming up. With his lightning-fast kung fu reflexes he took most of the fierce landing impact on his feet and sprawled out along his side unhurt.

But the wild maneuvering the truck had done in order to throw off Tommy sent it out of control at the top of another steep-raked hill with only a waist-high stone railing holding back the drop on one side. With ponderous slowness, the truck mounted the sidewalk, bounced into the stone railing, teetered over its edge and then toppled over, bashing itself into the street thirty feet below with a metallic thunderclap.

Tommy picked himself up. He spotted his gun in the gutter and returned it to his holster. Dashing to the stone railing, he saw the wheels spinning on the overturned car below. The crash hadn't started a fire or an explosion yet, but that could happen momentarily.

The pedestrian stairway down the hill was well away toward the bottom of the street and Tommy didn't take the time to use it. Instead he used the many handholds and footholds of the rough stone to clamber right down the side of the wall.

As he descended, he could see the unmoving forms of two gunmen lying lifeless by the truck. Both had been thrown through the cardboard-camouflaged open panel and one was partially pinned beneath the truck.

Tommy stepped down onto the sidewalk and rushed to the truck cab. Ben Moo Ling, the driver, was still barely alive. He lay crushed behind the steering wheel and was obviously in his last moments before death.

Still, he pulled together enough final energies to spit vainly in Tommy's direction. "We always knew you'd turn against your own people for a few dollars, you half-white bastard," gasped Moo Ling.

"My own people aren't anybody with yellow skins who try to shoot their way into a business conference of people who aren't bothering them," said Tommy. "What kind of a gang of crazy men would try something so bloodthirsty."

"You scumbag, you took the money of the Mafia against your own father's race," came the croaked reply.

"What Mafia?"

"Come off it. You know that meeting was a mob summit to try and figure out a way to hold their heroin monopoly and stop our brothers from bringing it in direct from Vietnam."

Tommy just stared at the dying man.

"Well, you're gonna get yours, you half-breed fink," grated Moo Ling with the death rattle starting to form. "The Thunder and Lightning gang will put you away for this. Nothing has stopped us yet, and before we're through we'll show the whole fucking world how oriental dudes are the toughest around. The Thunder and Lightning is gonna get you, Lee." And then he was dead.

The EWI truck was parked alongside the wreck, which

had now started to burn in the engine. Right behind was another EWI vehicle which had joined the chase, a Mustang convertible stationed a block from the mansion to serve as a runner.

Harry Chow came running over to Tommy. "What's going on, boss?" he demanded. "Are you okay?"

Tommy Lee's expression was grimly angry as he said, "You and the other guys wait here for the police. I'm taking the Mustang back to the mansion. It looks like the Delmonico family hasn't been exactly straight with us and I've got some questions they're going to answer."

CHAPTER FIVE

Tommy drove the Mustang back to the Pacific Heights mansion like a huge glob of slippery quicksilver. He cut through the quiet evening streets of San Francisco far over the legal speed limit but not to the point of being a maniac at the wheel.

He wanted to return to the Delmonicos as fast as possible, but challenging any patrol car that happened to be out on the streets was not the way to do it. So his eyes flicked continuously back and forth from the roadway to the rearview mirror to see if there were any police in the area.

At one point while crossing Van Ness he thought he saw a black-and-white police car a few blocks behind him. He immediately cut right at the next corner and kept whipping around corners until any possible pursuit would have been hopelessly lost. But all his slick maneuverings had been in the general direction of Pacific Heights and soon he was topping the hill before the gingerbread mansion where the chase had begun.

There was no sign of police or any guards out front now. Tommy cruised past and parked in the first available slot down the block. It was in front of a fire plug but EWI could afford a parking ticket.

Tommy ambled back to the gate with deceptive swiftness. Once he was standing outside the bars he could see the two guards waiting nervously in the shadows.

"Let me in, please," said Tommy. "I have an important message for Mr. Delmonico."

One of the guards pulled his hand out of the coat pocket and pointed a Colt .45 with a silencer at Tommy.

"We had some chinks here a little earlier with a message and a couple of my buddies got shot up pretty good," he said with a nasty chuckle. "Don't move, slant."

The other guard spoke a few words into a field telephone whose wires went into the house. In a few moments the front door opened and the craggy figure of Bill, the head house bodyguard, came looming toward the gate.

Bill glanced at Tommy and muttered to the guards, "It's okay. This is one of ours."

"I need to see Delmonico," said Tommy.

"Tomorrow. The meeting can't be interrupted tonight. Hey . . . what happened to the truck you were chasing?"

"It crashed. What happened to the guards' car that was shot up out here?"

"We moved it the hell out. What do you think? When the cops came all they had was some neighbors reporting they heard gunshots. They don't know if anyone got hit and as far as they can tell, there was a bunch of moving vehicles shooting it out. Nothing to do with this house."

"Okay, but what I have to tell Delmonico won't wait till morning. We found out something from the punks on the bakery truck that he'll want to know right away."

"No way I'm letting anybody inside during tonight's meeting. I got strict orders, including you. If you got any important information, tell me and I'll let Delmonico know."

"Sure," said Tommy, putting on a relieved smile. "But this is really hot stuff. C'mon over here and I'll whisper it to you."

The chief bodyguard grunted assent and pressed his burly body against the locked gate. Still smiling, Tommy leaned into the bars and reached up with one hand to put a friendly grip around Bill's thick neck.

Tommy looked into the other man's eyes as he squeezed. The bodyguard's eyes suddenly popped with excruciating pain and his mouth dropped open, yet somehow he couldn't scream or move. Only six feet away, the two other armed guards couldn't see that anything was wrong.

Tommy whispered into Bill's ear, "I'm going to let up on the grip a little. You'll be able to talk. Tell them to open the gate. Try anything and you'll be dead with a ruptured brain artery in twenty seconds." He pushed the man's head back, letting up slightly on his deadly judo nerve hold.

"You're right. . . . Mr. Delmonico will want to hear about this right away," Bill said in a tight, pinched voice. "Unlock the gate."

The closest guard unfastened the padlock that held the gate barred. He opened only one of the gate's two halves because Bill was standing in the way of the other one, still being clasped chummily around the neck by Tommy Lee.

Tommy could feel his captive tensing up to leap away. He let go in order to step around through the gate. Then it would be one unarmed man against three close-range guns. That's what Bill had been counting on.

But Tommy hadn't exactly forgotten he'd have to let go of the hostage to come inside.

For openers, he shifted his hold two inches downward and a little forward, then squeezed his fingers in for exactly one-third of a second. By moving his fingers off the death spot on the neck he only knocked Bill out instead of killing him.

As the chief guard started to fold up at the knees like an accordion, Tommy sprang forward in a lightning-like blur. Charging through the gate he took out the nearest guard with a kick in the pit of the stomach.

The two unconscious bodies hit the driveway almost in the same instant. Tommy stepped forward off the leg he'd kicked with as soon as it touched down. He was only a long stride away from the final guard, whose mouth was gaping open in shock and who was only just starting to bring up his weapon in aim at Tommy.

Tommy's hand slashed into the forearm holding the gun. The guard's paralyzed fingers let the weapon fall. Tommy bent sideways and swept his legs out from under him. He kicked the man at the base of the skull to ensure that he stayed out for some time, then walked back and did the same to the other two.

Satisfied, he walked briskly across the small lawn to the house and tried the front door. Finding it locked, he simply rang the bell.

Another tough opened it. He saw Tommy instead of Bill and all he had a chance to say was, "What?" Tommy slammed the door open into the guard's head with a thrust of his shoulder. The doorman sprawled backwards. Tommy sent him down with a heel-kick into the chest and moved on inside without breaking stride.

He was in a wide, high-ceilinged entrance hall with marble floors, a room out of the grand past of American social privilege. There were three hoods with carbines seated at the sides of the room, two at one wall and the other opposite.

"Stop!" yelled one of the hall guards, brandishing his carbine rifle as the other two chimed in with variations like "Freeze!" and "Halt!"

Tommy grinned and said, "I'll let you throw your guns down if you don't want to get hurt." He turned left and moved toward the wall with the two gunmen as bullets began to burp harmlessly all around him.

Of course, Tommy was advancing in an extremely special way. He was doing the legendary Ninja walk, the movement of the fabled Japanese assassin cult which was reputed to have the power to make itself invisible.

Ninjutsu's mystical but highly practicable techniques had been believed lost for over a century until they were rediscovered and unified into the modern martial art of aikido by great Japanese masters like Ueshiba, who could disarm a crack shot firing at him point blank or from fifty yards away—at the age and poundage of eighty-five.

What Tommy was doing was the Dance of the Eight Directions, a wildly complex maneuver that he had learned at the Tokyo studio of the family Ueshiba as a teenager. He bobbed and stepped, slid and pivoted, leaned and bounced. If he had been doing the eight-movement routine on the same spot, it would have required sixty-four separate motions before he returned to his original position.

However, Tommy was definitely not remaining in one

small area. Rather, he was gliding across the smooth floor toward two rapid-firing riflemen, moving like he had somehow churned himself into butter.

It was an art beyond dancing. Tommy was one of the few persons in the world who had mastered this remarkable skill to the point where he could actually make himself appear transparent in motion. He was truly as safe in a field of flying bullets as a baby sleeping in a cradle. The best chance the gunmen would have had of hitting him was to simply shut their eyes and fire at random, taking a chance on the astronomical odds against getting him with a stray bullet. The movements of the Dance of the Eight Directions made it impossible to take true aim at the target.

But not everybody else in the room was as safe as Tommy Lee. He maneuvered himself in front of the single gunner behind him, during a point when he was facing partially away from the two he was advancing toward. He slowed down his dance just enough so that the duo thought they at last had a reasonably accurate fix on him.

Then he swirled aside as the two opened up and blasted a stream of bullets into their comrade behind Tommy.

By the time Tommy was nine feet away from the two riflemen, one of them had already emptied his clip and was trying frantically to reload while gibbering with rage, frustration, and fear.

Tommy came in from the side that kept the reloading gunman shielding him from the other foe. He lashed out with his heel and sent the closest hood sprawling into the other one. Then he sprang forward with both hands slashing and cut them down in instants.

Calmly, hardly breathing fast, Tommy turned to survey the room and choose where to go next. He looked up when he heard the sound of applause above him.

Standing along the railing of the balcony above him were Bartlett and Lisa Delmonico and about a dozen expensively dressed middle-aged men. The suave Bartlett Delmonico was leading the clapping.

"Astonishing, Mr. Lee," he said. "A remarkable display. I've never seen anything like it. I had no idea such a thing was possible."

"Oh, it's very possible," said Tommy. "Are we going to be able to do some straight talking now, or do you have some more hired guns you'd like me to put away for you."

"By all means, let's talk," said Delmonico. "If I'd had any conception that you were so astoundingly lethal, I'd never have left orders to keep you out of the way for the rest of the night." So saying, he led the group down the sweeping curve of stairs that went down to the entry hall.

Tommy scanned the faces of the group as Delmonico approached, with Lisa close at his side. The girl looked cool and stunning in a tailored suede pants-suit. But right now it was the other men's faces in the crowd that he was most interested in.

Did he recognize any of them? That's what was important. None of the men in the front rank was familiar to him. And then he spotted in the middle of the knot of people a face that had been in hundreds of newspaper photos—Big Joe Calabria, the Mafia boss of Philadelphia.

And a few feet behind him was Needles Marconi, a mobster operating out of Reno. And next to him was Florida narcotics kingpin Roland Bocaccio.

The dying words of Ben Moo Ling had been true. This so-called business conference was in fact a high-level meeting of the American Mafia.

"Since there probably won't be any more attacks tonight, let's go into the den and be comfortable," said Delmonico. He led the way through a corridor off the entry hall.

The den was like one of those comfortably manly exclusive clubs that gentlemen detectives used to hang out in during mystery novels written earlier in the century. There was a brick fireplace in action, a well-stocked bar and a lot of leather chairs and couches placed throughout the room.

Delmonico's crew took places in the seats. Tommy remained standing, with his back against a wall of bookshelves.

"Do you want to introduce yourselves?" he asked the group. "I recognize Mr. Calabria, Mr. Marconi, and Mr. Bocaccio. Probably the names of most of the rest of you would be professionally familiar to me also. How about you, Mr. Delmonico? Who are you, really?"

Delmonico was at the bar, shaking up martinis for himself and Lisa. "My name *is* Bartlett Delmonico. Legally and for a long time. I do live in Bermuda and I am a financier by trade."

"But your financiering is done with mob money," said Tommy.

"Of course. The whole world must be run by specialists these days. Why should our brotherhood be any different. I'm in the investment end of our operations, that and management consulting. It's up to others to run the field operations, which is why I've never had the problem of bad publicity."

"Or prison terms," added Tommy. "But why drag me and EWI into whatever it is you're doing here?"

"Why not? You run a detective agency and we were in legitimate need of your specialized services. As you saw tonight, we've had a very real threat to this conference by a gang of oriental extortionists. Which brings us to the point . . . what happened to the Chinese hoodlums whose truck you were chasing?"

"They died in a crash. But one of them lived long enough to accuse me of selling out my own people to work for the Mafia, helping you protect your heroin pipeline against competition from Southeast Asia. I didn't like hearing that and I came back here to find out if it was true. I expect I know the answer already. And I don't like it. I also don't like being lied to when I'm hired for a case."

"Of course it's true," said Delmonico. "And we lied to you because we needed you and that was the only way to get you. What else would you expect from us?"

"That's all I needed to know, Mr. Delmonico," said Tommy. "I'm resigning from your case as of now. You'll get the bill for tonight's surveillance. But from now on this meeting is on its own."

"Isn't it against your professional ethics to quit a case you've accepted?" asked Delmonico.

"Don't make me sick by trying a Mafia ethics lecture," said Tommy. "When you withheld true facts, you cleared me of any responsibility to protect you."

"That might not be such a healthy idea for you," said the glowering Philadelphia boss, Big Joe Calabria.

"Please, Daddy," Lisa Delmonico interrupted quickly.

Tommy turned to the girl. "Daddy?" he said. "How many daddys do you have around here? Or is that just an honorary term?"

Lisa shot him a vicious stare while Bartlett Delmonico burst out laughing and Calabria reached under his jacket.

"Go ahead, darling," Delmonico laughed. "Tell him."

"I was born Lisa Calabria," she said proudly. "The heir to an old and mighty tradition. To the outside world, Bartlett Delmonico pretends he's my father so that we both have greater freedom to accomplish the many complex things we must do. But I have the honor to say he is really my beloved husband."

She stood there among all the men with the haughty, aggressive stance of some modern-day Lucretia Borgia, a true princess of power politics for whom mastery of events was the ultimate thrill.

"We want you to stay on the job, Lee," said Delmonico. "This Thunder and Lightning outfit is a menace that must be dealt with severely, even if they are your people. Tell us what kind of money you want, we'll make it worth your while."

"You don't understand. I'm not for hire to any murderers, robbers, or dope pushers. I don't give a damn whether it's you old-time syndicate creeps or some hungry punks who have a skin color similar to mine. As far as I'm concerned, the best thing that could happen for the world would be if the Mafia and the Thunder and Lightning mob blew each other's brains out. I wouldn't dream of getting in the way of your gang war. As a matter of fact, I told my men not to tell the police anything about the overturned attack truck except that they reported an accident. Have a nice bloodbath, gentlemen. I am leaving now."

Before he could take a step toward the door, Bartlett Delmonico said, "Lee, we can't find the Thunder and Lightning gang in Chinatown, so you're going to do it for us. We are not about to let some runty hoodlums interfere with the billions of dollars in the heroin market. You've got exactly forty-eight hours to find the gang and show us how to put them out of business. Or else you will be personally responsible for the deaths of a lot of innocent bystanders.

"Oh yeah, how do you figure that, Mr. Financier?"

"Very simple. If you don't bring us the leaders of Thunder and Lightning in forty-eight hours, we will start taking three random hostages every day on the streets of Chinatown and shooting them down. The police will think it's only another outbreak of your wild new Chinese gang violence. You get us what we want, Lee, or we'll start killing off your people."

CHAPTER SIX

The comings and goings were building up to a crescendo the next afternoon at the high, narrow building that was central community headquarters for the tongs in San Francisco's Chinatown.

The building was a modern job, designed to look oriental. It was always covered with the banners of the member tong clans and it held a power over the citizens of Chinatown that few outsiders were even aware of.

True, the Chinese-American tongs were no longer the invisible government they had been up to about forty years ago. For the early waves of Chinese immigrants to the U.S., the tongs played as important a part in their lives as the official American government—perhaps an even more important part.

Brought over to build the railroads across the West for a few cents an hour, the hard-working Chinese had left their women and families at home far away. They were faced with a new language totally different from their native tongue, among rough and unsympathetic strangers who often considered them not quite human.

No wonder these early Chinese-Americans fell back on the great strength of their people for organizing as a cooperative community.

The tongs had existed as super-family clans for centuries, of course. It was simply a matter of transferring their organizational lines wherever in the world emigrant Chinese communities sprung up.

No other people have anything like the Chinese tongs. Not exactly extended families, not exactly fraternal organizations, not exactly business firms, legal aid societies, social clubs, or religious orders—yet the tongs were a little bit of all of these and more.

Membership was basically by bloodlines. All the Lees, Wus, Fongs, Chings, and the rest had their own far-spread name clans. Tommy Lee would automatically have far more in common with somebody else sharing his last name than with another Chinese. Still of course the foreign Chinese stuck together for mutual defense against the outsiders.

Originally, the tongs were probably formed to give traveling merchants a protective web of organization in the far-flung cities of old China as commerce began to grow and communications were slow from village to village.

At the height of their glory, the tongs were the main channels of Chinese commerce around the world. Great merchant empires were set up along tong lines and the ordinary Chinese generally owed more of their livelihoods to the tong chieftains than to the Emperors in faraway Peking.

But as always, whenever there were great concentrations of power and wealth competing among themselves, great and violent struggles arose. By the beginning of the twentieth century, wealth was flowing into coffers of the tongs from a network of émigré workers and Chinatowns around the world. Oriental merchandise was flowing around the world to be distributed from the Chinatowns in increasingly lucrative quantities.

Old business and personal feuds grew and were shipped to new locations along with the valuable goods. Finally these secret battles erupted into great gangwars in city after city around the time of World War I. For almost two decades, the expression Tong War was as familiar to all Americans and Europeans as Mafia would be today.

The dreaded figure of the hatchet man, a superbly trained and bloodthirsty assassin who struck down his victims in silence and shadow, became a figure of popular culture as well known as the hit-man killer of today.

And at last there were no spoils left for the tongs to war over. The modern corporation and newer technology watered down the power of tong-style international organization.

But the tongs didn't disappear entirely. Instead of robber barons, they retained portions of their power as communal organizations looking out for the basic interests of their vast memberships. Not nearly as exciting as the old days, but not nearly as bloody.

As Chinese-Americans became increasingly accepted into the fabric of national life, there was no longer a need for such services as tong-operated schools and clinics. Still, the Chinese reverence for tradition is well known and tongs remained a vast central part of life in the Chinatowns of the world.

That's why Tommy Lee knew he had absolutely no chance of tracking down and destroying the mysterious new Thunder and Lightning mob without the all-out aid of the tongs of San Francisco.

He had left the Delmonico mansion shortly after hearing the Mafia ultimatum, returned to his office and immediately started making calls to the tong leaders. He slept for a few hours at the office, took a shower in the morning and changed clothes from the wardrobe he maintained at all branches of East-West Investigations.

Then he at once renewed his efforts to reach the tong chiefs council members. By mid-morning he was out on the streets of Chinatown, sipping endless cups of tea and nibbling endless exotic tidbits as he went from restaurant to restaurant where the wise old leaders of the tongs might be found.

Tommy Lee was calling a Dragon Alarm, a most serious and rare occurence in the Chinese communities. The last such Dragon Alarm conference had been at the time when the U.S. was finally prepared to give full diplomatic recognition to Communist China, an event which would obviously have wide repercussions throughout the entire Chinese-American community as old loyalties became subject to sweeping changes.

Previous Dragon Alarm meetings had been held when the Japanese attacked Pearl Harbor, when North Korea attacked South Korea and when Mao's Communists took over China. In each case, alternatives were discussed and a common policy eventually decided on so that every person in Chinatown understood where his ultimate loyalties should go.

There were currently twenty-three active tongs in San Francisco and the official leaders of nineteen were in town today. Alternate representatives had been found to speak for the rest.

Tommy sat by the front table in the central tong headquarters main conference room and watched the grave-faced elders of San Francisco's Chinatown start to come filing in. The meeting was to start in a few minutes, at 4:00 p.m.

Tommy already knew most of the central tong council and he bowed politely to each man as he entered. Generally, the tong chiefs were the most wealthy and powerful merchants of the community. But this was not always the case, a number of tongs were led by small businessmen who were revered for their knowledge and wisdom, rather than their abilities to make a great deal of money.

Such a man was Lo Sing, president of the tong council, who was now entering the room, surrounded by respectful followers. Lo Sing was a frail, serene-looking man who owned a small grocery store that sold imported Chinese delicacies. But he spent most of his time deeply involved in the cares of the teeming Chinatown district, using his great wisdom to help others rather than himself in the true tradition of the Chinese sage.

Slowly Lo Sing made his way across the room, stopped every few feet by another greeting from a tong leader. Many conversations were going on throughout the conference hall, lively and animated as always when groups of Chinese got together.

But the chattering talk ended in an instant when Lo Sing got to the front table and held up his hand for silence. "My brothers, this is a most grave and serious occasion. The lives of our people have been threatened by a cruel and vicious outside force. We must decide what is best to do about it."

A gabble of suggestions in various Chinese dialects

greeted this opening announcement. Lo Sing held up his hand again. "First let us hear the entire story from our young colleague, Tommy Lee. We must have all the information before we make decisions."

Tommy stepped forward and gazed over the rows of faces crowded before him. In fluent and polished Chinese, he said, "Thank you, most venerable and revered Lo Sing for allowing my unworthy self to address this mighty gathering. I thank all of you tong chiefs also for accepting my judgment about the seriousness of this threat against our people and coming here today in answer to my Dragon Alarm."

Any of Tommy's American friends, who knew him only as a flashy and wisecracking private investigator, would have been shocked to hear him talking with such flowery respect to a group of elderly businessmen.

But not for nothing had Tommy Lee been raised in the firm Asiatic tradition of respect for elders. Lifetime experience still counted far more to Chinese than it does to Americans. Tommy knew that the men seated before him controlled more than the bulk of the money in Chinatown. They controlled thousands of human allegiances in these crowded streets.

The central tong council could order thousands of eyes to look for signs of the Thunder and Lightning gang, they could send thousands of legs out on the streets to carry back answers.

And Tommy had been well taught in the language and approach to properly communicate with such powerful elder statesmen. It was one reason why he was so outstandingly successful as a detective in the Orient.

"Briefly, for those of you who do not already know, I was hired under false pretenses by a council of Mafia bosses who are meeting here to defend their monopoly of the American heroin business. They claimed to me that they were legitimate businessmen who had been threatened by a gang of Chinese extortionists to have their conference disrupted if they didn't pay off. When I found out the truth, I confronted the mobsters and was told that if I didn't deliver them the leaders of this Thunder and Lightning gang within forty-eight hours, they would start shooting down innocent Chinese hostages on the streets. This is the crisis our community is facing."

"The men of the Mafia are desperate to keep Asiatic heroin from coming into America and taking away the millions upon millions of dollars they make from this horrible death drug," said Lo Sing. "They would indeed do anything to stop their rivals."

"I feel that your words are absolutely correct, wise tong master," said Tommy. "We here know what the Mafia is and that they can be expected to live up to their threat. But what do we know of the Thunder and Lightning? It seems to be a most secret organization and I seek the help of a Dragon Alarm council to learn how to deal with them properly."

"Quite so, young Lee," answered the council president. Lo Sing was not really an old man, no older than in his early sixties, it was the authority of his personality that gave him the presence of an elder statesman. "I do not believe any single one of us knows a great deal about the Thunder and Lightning. So therefore let us now combine what we do know. For myself, I began to hear of this Thunder and Lightning perhaps six months ago. And it was my understanding that the gang was formed overseas before branching out to San Francisco."

"Yes, I heard of Thunder and Lightning in Southeast Asia a year ago," said a wisp-thin old man with a white chin-beard. "They were smugglers and robbers, most fierce."

A fat man in a blue suit chimed in, "There are a few young men in San Francisco reputed to be members of the Thunder and Lightning. But they have dropped out of sight. Only those who keep their membership hidden are at large in Chinatown."

Another man said, "This gang is not made up of petty criminals who seek thrills, like so many of the others that are giving us trouble here. The Thunder and Lightning is something new. Not only are they very tough and ruthless, they are extremely well organized and clearly they are operating with some big overall plan in mind, perhaps involving a heroin network from Southeast Asia."

Lo Sing said, "A picture is beginning to emerge, do you all agree?" There were shouts of assent and he went on. "The business of enslaving human beings to heroin is disgusting. But it becomes even worse if the shame of controlling heroin in America passes on to the Chinese people. Then it is a shame for all of us, all of the tongs."

"We can't let that happen," shouted the bearded old man who had spoken earlier.

"Yes, the first order of importance is to ensure that Chinese do not become the heroin merchants," said Lo Sing. "And for that reason, we can even accept a temporary alliance with the evil men of the Mafia. But we do not join with the Mafia at the point of their guns, not the tongs. Tommy Lee, how would it be if you told the gangsters something like this . . .?"

Tommy's voice was cheerful when he got on the phone to the Delmonico rented mansion early that evening. He got through two wary flunkies before Lisa came on the line. "I have a counteroffer for you," he told her.

Lisa gave a warm, throaty laugh over the phone that contrasted weirdly with her chilling words. "You don't seem to understand, Lee. This isn't any bargaining session. You're going to do exactly what you were ordered to do or we start killing hostages on the streets of Chinatown."

"You're not dealing with a full deck anymore, sweetheart," said Tommy, easily reverting to his usual bantering Americanized style. "There's a new player. I am no longer speaking just for myself and EWI. I have a message to pass on from the Central Tong Association of San Francisco."

"The tongs?" Lisa said warily.

"Yes, we're still very much in the tong business in Chinatown . . . even if we have phased out our hatchets in favor of guns and politics. I have some good news for you and some bad news. Which do you want first?"

"Don't play games. Get on with it."

"The good news is that we want to get rid of the Thunder and Lightning as badly as you do."

"Then I don't see that there's anything more to say. What's the point of this call?"

"The bad news is that if you don't do it our way, everybody at your famous meeting is going to leave San Francisco either dead or in FBI handcuffs." There was a pause at the other end of the line and Tommy added, "I'm not just saying this to hear myself talk."

"Come on over to the mansion now," said Lisa.

"That's what I had in mind," Tommy told her.

Tommy drove back to Pacific Heights and was passed on into the mansion without any difficulties. The elite gathering of international Mafia chiefs was waiting in assemblage at the club-like library room.

By way of greeting, Bartlett Delmonico said, "We don't take ultimatums, young man." Lisa sat in an armchair near her husband, her eyes glittering with excitement.

"That's up to you," said Tommy. "But the tongs don't push around easy either. How would you like an offer you can't refuse?"

Lisa said, "That would be quite interesting if you could bring it off."

"Well, here's the way it goes. There isn't going to be any more discussion about grabbing Chinatown hostages. That idea goes into the shitcan. Or you get total war on all fronts. The tongs vs. the Mafia. Not just in San Francisco but in every Chinatown around the world. You're not going to buy us off like you do with law enforcement. We'll be out to break up your systems from top to bottom. Whatever it takes, the tongs have enough manpower to do it. And when the San Francisco Central Council speaks, they're talking for all the Chinatowns. The first hostage goes and you've got war."

"How the hell did the tongs get into this, Lee?" growled Delmonico. "You know what we do to double-crossers."

"Double-crossing has nothing to do with it. If the Thunder and Lightning wasn't so well-hidden and deeply entrenched, you wouldn't need a specialist to get at them.

I knew up front that I couldn't track them down without the tongs' Chinatown network. So I had to go to the Central Council. After all, they don't want innocent Chinese getting killed. What better reason for cooperating?"

"But they will cooperate. Isn't that the point?" Lisa countered.

"Sure, we'll cooperate with anything that stops Thunder and Lightning. The tongs don't want Chinese taking over the heroin trade and losing face for all our people. That's top priority. We can work together on this. Just forget about that hostage deadline and there's no need to fight each other at this point."

"All right," said Delmonico, "just so we see progress being made within a reasonable time. There won't be any problem. Go ahead and get to work. I want a report every twelve hours."

"Sure." But Tommy didn't make any move to leave just yet. "There's only one more thing."

"Well . . . ?"

"It'll cost you one million dollars."

The roomful of Mafia leaders exploded into a shouting pandemonium. "A million bucks . . . up yours." "What is this crap?" "No way, punk." "Try and get it." These were some of the less obscene responses.

Tommy waited until the noise died down and they stopped shaking their fists at him. "The million dollars is for a new community center in Chinatown. The tongs feel we need more facilities to keep young guys doing something constructive and staying out of gangs. See, we're helping you avoid competition. Isn't that what you want?"

"We have less expensive ways of stopping competition," said Delmonico.

"I'm sure you do. But the plain fact is that neither you nor I can root out Thunder and Lightning without the tongs. They're making a fair charge for their services, considering that's the only way you can keep the status quo, it seems. The million dollars is payable thirty days from the dissolution of the T and L. . . . It'll wind up costing you a lot more if you don't pay up."

Delmonico glanced around the room and apparently

read an answer in the eyes of his associates. "It's a deal," he said. "Just get us the Thunder and Lightning gang."

"With their heads on a platter, if you like," said Tommy.

He got up to leave, not wanting to be around these people any longer than necessary. But then Lisa Delmonico was calling to him, "Wait a moment, Mr. Lee. I'll get you our file on the Thunder and Lightning. It's not much but it might be of some help."

Tommy recognized her tone of voice and the look in her eyes, however. He had seen it the day before in the upstairs bedroom when Lisa threw herself into sex with him. It wasn't any file she wanted to lay on Tommy now.

CHAPTER SEVEN

"Follow me, please," Lisa Delmonico said as she led Tommy out of the meeting room. She was very businesslike indeed, and only the slight extra flounce of her delicious bottom signaled to Tommy Lee that the kinky beauty had more than official business in mind.

They left the den and walked past the corridor guards into a smaller study that had been converted into an office by the setting up of file cabinets and a desk.

Lisa flung the door shut behind Tommy. There was a light switch by the knob but she ignored it and instead snapped the bolt into place. With her dark eyes blazing she locked gazes with Tommy and said matter-of-factly, "I want to fuck. Right now."

"In the old country, a lady usually says, 'I want to be fucked,'" said Tommy.

"Do you want to discuss comparative sociology or do you want to get it on?" Lisa demanded. She pulled her blue, shiny dress up over her hips. She was wearing sky-blue panties with two embroidered valentines at one side.

"I'll show you what I want to do," said Tommy.

His arm flicked out like a rapier and he tugged at her panties for the briefest of instants. When he let go, the blue silk triangle was still there but his fingers had sliced a neat slit up the middle.

Tommy placed his hands around the pliant waist of the girl and lifted her easily. He sat down on a two-drawer metal file case and placed Lisa across his thighs with her legs straddling him.

She said, "I guess I don't have to tell you I get turned on by power struggles, by the conflict of strong wills." She laughed and started to unfasten Tommy's pants with clinical precision. "I almost came on the spot when you told the capos it would cost them a million dollars."

"That *was* pretty good," Tommy agreed. "And so is this." Lisa had worked his member out of the layers of cloth sheaths. And now she gripped it firmly and stroked it. Only a few strokes were required before the penis was fully aroused and towering erect.

Without any ado, the elegant Lisa Delmonico hitched herself up and mounted the rod, smiling enigmatically as the golden shaft thrust through the slit in her panties.

Immediately she began bouncing up and down, working up to high speed within moments. Her breathing came in heavy gasps. Tommy moved along with her underlying rhythm, not trying to keep up with her frantic speed but helping support the major thrusts.

With only this elementary assistance from Tommy, Lisa rapidly worked herself into the frenzy of orgasm and her body shuddered uncontrollably as she dug her fingernails into his shoulders. Her eyes rolled wildly and she gave a deep sigh of relief.

Tommy said, "Now that you're through using me as a human vibrator, let me show you where it's at."

He commenced a smoothly pulsating movement that was unhurried, yet it more than equalled in intensity of sensation the frantic squirmings with which Lisa had gotten herself off. The girl was blasé about this new approach at first. But as Tommy's smooth, insistent movement kept coming on and on, she began to get drawn into the abandon of lovemaking again.

Tommy swirled his pelvis while maintaining his back and forth rocking patterns. He put an arch into his loins that was the final touch to the legendary snake motion of Chinese sex lore.

"Stop it, I can't stand any more," Lisa was screaming. "Please, I beg you." And then she came apart, her limbs twitching spasmodically as Tommy's hot seed finally spouted into her.

Tommy had to hold her up to keep her from falling

over in a dead faint. As for him, it took only a few deep meditation breaths till he regained his serenity.

"Did you want to let me have that file now?" he asked.

"File?"

"The Thunder and Lightning file. Remember?"

"Oh that!" She staggered over to sit heavily down in the office chair. "I ... forget where I put it. I'll send it over later by a messenger."

"Thanks," said Tommy casually as he left. "It's a pleasure doing business with you." The armed guards nearby in the corridor were having fits trying to keep their faces straight after hearing the passionate sounds of love-making from inside the office.

Whistling cheerfully, Tommy exited the Mafia conference mansion and drove back to Chinatown, watching carefully in his Jaguar's rearview mirror to see that no raiding teams from the Thunder and Lightning had followed him from Pacific Heights.

A bright, medium-sized meeting room on one of the upper floors of the central tong headquarters had been commandeered for use as the central point in the search for the mysterious Thunder and Lightning gang. The place was a bustling beehive of activity, with rows of folding tables lined up as workdesks along the walls.

About a dozen Chinese of all ages and descriptions were hard at work behind the desks, shuffling growing piles of notepaper into neatly increasing piles. Runners kept dashing in and out of the room with new bits of information that were duly inscribed on the notepapers by someone at a desk. A porcelain pot of the everpresent Chinese tea was on a shielded hotplate in the corner.

In charge of all this cauldron of activity was Lo Sing himself, president of the tong council. Grasping a thick sheaf of papers, Lo Sing bustled over to Tommy and said, "Welcome, young friend. The work goes well, I think."

"Greetings, most venerable father," said Tommy with flowery formality. "May I ask what has been done, so far?"

"Of course. It would seem that our first step must be to create a file of all persons believed to be part of the

Thunder and Lightning as well as all the suspects' associates in Chinatown. This is being done as speedily as possible."

"Alas, I am afraid the file has not yet turned up the whereabouts of one active gang member yet, or you would have told me about it. Am I not right?"

"Unfortunately you are indeed right," sighed Lo Sing. "But what I have here are our finest pearls of information to date. For example, only moments ago we were brought the address of the mother of a young rascal named Bobby Hu, who is believed to have disappeared into the Thunder and Lightning underground several months ago."

"Yes, Bobby Hu, I remember him from the teen gangs," mused Tommy. "I knew his mother and the entire family well."

"I thought this was the case," said Lo Sing. "Perhaps you would choose to question good Mother Hu yourself."

"Yes, at once," said Tommy. "But have you come yet to any theory about how these punks like Bobby Hu all manage to drop from sight so completely after their membership in the Thunder and Lightning is discovered? Chinatown is a crowded place and it would be impossible to hide so many young men here."

Lo Sing smiled, "I fear you are trying to test my wits, young brother. You see the only answer as clearly as I do."

"Forgive me, honored Lo Sing. It is only a habit of my trade to seek to lead others into saying what you already suspect and to perhaps add more significant details. As you do, I understand that the Thunder and Lightning lair must be outside of Chinatown. There is nothing noticeable today about young Chinese taking homes anywhere in the cities. I only wondered if you had yet any clue as to which direction the hidden gang members have gone."

To this, Lo Sing could only shake his head sadly.

Before anything else could happen, a postman came in with a special delivery letter. He was a big black man and he looked about amusedly at this roomful of busily scurrying Chinese. "What is this, a convention?" he asked.

"Sort of," said Tommy. "What've you got?"

"Are you Mr. Lo Sing?"

"That is myself," said the council president. The postman handed him a fat envelope and walked off chuckling. "A convention," he muttered to himself.

"Perhaps this is some useful information from an anonymous source," said Lo Sing, starting to peel back the flap of the envelope.

Suddenly there was something about the thick outline of the envelope that struck Tommy as suspiciously familiar. He had seen similar envelopes before in the Far East—and people had died from opening them.

"Stop," he shouted wildly and in the same instant he snatched the envelope out of Lo Sing's hand with one of his blinding fast kung fu motions.

As Lo Sing and all the others in the room stared incredulously, Tommy swiftly ran his fingers over the envelope, pressing lightly and carefully. Yes, there was the faint shape of hard objects outlined under the carefully hollowed-out sheathing of papers. And there was the telltale micro-line of wire under the flap.

"This is a Hong Kong letter bomb," Tommy announced. "They make those things for the whole Orient."

He walked quickly to the oversized teapot, removed the lid and dumped the letter inside. The tong volunteers gathered around while Tommy counted off two minutes on his gold Pulsar digital watch.

He pulled out the drenched envelope and let it drip a moment into the teapot. Then he poked his finger through the wet middle of the paper and started peeling it apart.

First he disconnected the thin slice of plastic explosive from the soaked and disarmed fuse, the next step was to let the trigger spring snap shut. These deadly components had been tucked into holes cut to their shape inside the folded roll of blank stationery.

"The main thing about a well-made letter bomb is that it has to stand up under post office rough handling and only explode when the envelope is opened," said Tommy. "That's why they're easy to disarm once you spot them."

And then he saw the folded square of parchment nestled inside the paper with the bomb parts. He opened the parchment, read the curt message written there, and handed it over to Lo Sing who read it aloud.

The note said, "So you have been lucky this time, old fools and a young turncoat. Otherwise you would not be reading this warning. Beware of the Thunder and Lightning. We will strike you again and again unless you stop trying to hunt us down through Chinatown like jungle beasts. The Thunder and Lightning does not sit waiting defenselessly while traitors seek to exterminate us."

Lo Sing put down the parchment and said, "So this is war now. The tongs against the madmen of the Thunder and Lightning. Then it must be. They dare to strike against the chosen leaders of their own people. We must wipe them out forever."

"All right," said Tommy. "Now we see we must all keep a sharp watch for more sneak attacks by these killers."

"We start the battle," said Lo Sing. "There can be no safety for anyone in Chinatown until Thunder and Lightning is destroyed."

"My own next part in this battle will be to reconnoiter the domicile of the family, wise Lo Sing," said Tommy. "If you would be so kind as to give me the address..."

Tommy whizzed through the cluttered streets of Chinatown on the most effective form of fast transportation in a traffic-choked city. It was a glossy black Honda 750 motorcycle, a big, wickedly powerful machine as fast and maneuverable as anything on the road.

He'd had one of his operatives at EWI bring over the bike to the tong council building and it was waiting for him inside the lobby under the watchful eye of another EWI sentry Tommy had posted at the door.

Tommy felt good with the early evening breeze cooling his face. His thoughts turned to memories of childhood days with the neighboring Hu family. Mrs. Hu had bravely raised the five children herself after her husband died of cancer while still young. Wearing herself down year after year in a series of grueling jobs—laundry worker, cook, seamstress—she raised one son into an accountant, another as a lawyer, and two daughters as contented housewives. Bobby Hu, the next-to-youngest, had always been the wild misfit in this classic lifting-by-your-own-bootstraps classic American immigrant success story.

At first Bobby was just a reckless kid who stood out by his brashness from the disciplined, quiet rest of the family. But as he went on into his teens, a more sinister pattern emerged. Unable to conform to the demands of school and his community, Bobby became a feared central figure in the growing youth-gang subculture of San Francisco's Chinatown.

But still, this was a long way from the all-out near-suicidal desperation which seemed the hallmark of the mysterious Thunder and Lightning gang. How had Bobby Hu crossed the line from roughneck to bloodthirsty outcast?

In a few moments he halted the throbbing cycle by a typically old, high, and narrow apartment house on a typically steep-hilled San Francisco street. He beckoned over a group of alert-eyed youngsters who had been playing penny-toss against the wall nearby and told them he'd pay a dollar for them to keep watch on the Honda superbike. With the Thunder and Lightning on the warpath, it would be too easy for them to attack by sabotaging his motorcycle.

He climbed the musty but clean steps to the third floor and knocked at the door at the end of the hall. In rapid-fire Canton Chinese, a gruff female voice from inside demanded to know who was there.

Tommy announced himself in impeccable dialect pronunciation and immediately the clicking of multiple latches being unbarred began. But still the last doorchain was left in place as Mrs. Hu peeked through the crack to make sure the visitor was really who he claimed to be. In this era of high crime, with the elderly and alone as the most perfect victims, suspicion becomes survival and normal behavior.

But once Tommy had stepped inside the homey little apartment, the welcome he received from his old childhood friend was as warm and genuine as anyone could have asked. Mrs. Hu threw her arms around him and her eyes were bright with happy tears as she chattered on in Chinese about how good it was to see Tommy and how well he looked.

After a few moments the flood of greetings stopped and the lonely but proud old lady said, "A busy and important man like Tommy Lee has become would not have time to visit a foolish old lady like me unless there was some business you need me for."

Tommy replied gallantly, "My business is I was thinking how much I missed your home-baked tea cookies and I couldn't stand not having them any more." They both knew he was fibbing, but this was the kind of polite pretense expected in Chinese society.

"Of course you must have some tea and cookies at once," said Mrs. Hu. "Sit right down and tell me how things are with you."

"I would rather hear about how your children are," smiled Tommy. "We were all such good friends as children.

Mrs. Hu bustled busily around the crowded apartment, brewing a fresh pot of tea and warming a batch of her deliciously fluffy cookies in the stove. Her satisfaction was evident as she rattled on glowingly about her two successful sons and happily married daughters.

But she said nothing of her fifth child. "And what about Bobby?" Tommy prompted her. "Is the poor guy still getting in and out of trouble?"

Mrs. Hu gave a curt nod, more to herself than Tommy. Now she knew what the true purpose of this visit was. "Unfortunately, it has become necessary for me to think of Bobby as dead. Not that I love Bobby any less, despite what he has become. But he is beyond doubt doomed. And he will be killed before too long. It is too painful to continue hoping otherwise."

She set down the teapot and a plate of cookies before Tommy. "My Bobby is an outcast. He has cut himself off from everybody, even the wild teen gangs he used to run with. Only a breed of others as desperate as he will now associate with him. . . . I suppose Bobby has done something very bad and you are now hunting him, the way Tommy Lee has become so famous for hunting men."

"I don't know if Bobby has done anything. It's the Thunder and Lightning gang I'm looking for. And Bobby Hu is one of the few people known to be connected with it."

Mrs. Hu poured out the first cup of tea and Tommy said, "How could Bobby become part of something as insanely evil as the Thunder and Lightning? These maniacs must be stopped from doing something terrible—with drugs from Asia—that would bring great shame on all our people in America."

"I'm not surprised," said Mrs. Hu. "When Bobby stole the saved-up treasury of his teen gang in order to buy a Cadillac and mink coat to impress his white girlfriend, I knew he had no honor left. He had turned on those to whom he swore loyalty, even though it was the loyalty of gangsters. They searched for him and would have killed him if he was found in Chinatown. And then I heard Bobby was recruited for the Thunder and Lightning, who accept only those who are outcasts everywhere else."

"I don't suppose you know where Bobby is?"

"Of course not." Mrs. Hu wiped at her eyes.

"Do you ever see him? Does he come here?"

Mrs. Hu hesitated before answering. "Sometimes he comes here," she said at last. "I never know when. Usually it seems to be just before the Thunder and Lightning is about to put him into some great danger."

"Has he come to you recently?" Tommy demanded.

"No. Not for at least two months. Maybe he won't come again." Her voice started to break. "Maybe Bobby is dead already."

Maybe he was, Tommy thought. But in case Bobby Hu was still at large, certainly the start of a great heroin war ought to be the sort of danger that would bring him in to see his mother one more time. EWI would have to put a watch on this apartment at once.

Meanwhile, there were perhaps a few more things he could find out here. "What about Bobby's girlfriend?" he asked. "The one he stole the gang treasury for? Are they still lovers?"

"That I do not know."

"What's her name?"

"Rosie ... Rosalie. Something like that. She was a topless dancer at some of the go-go bars where Chinatown meets North Beach. Later, I heard she stopped dancing and was a cocktail waitress at these bars. She's not really a bad person, I suppose. She didn't know where Bobby stole the money to get her those things."

"Thank you, Mother Hu," said Tommy. "I won't ask you anything else." He reached for one of her fluff-light cookies, glad of the chance to visit with a dear old friend for a few minutes with no more unhappy questions to bring up.

And then the door to the apartment was being unlocked swiftly by someone who had the proper keys. When the door was open, standing there was Bobby Hu.

He and Tommy stared at each other for an instant. Then Hu's hand darted under his coat. He whipped out a pistol and brought it into aim at Tommy.

CHAPTER EIGHT

Tommy Lee did not just sit there and wait to be gunned down as Bobby brought up his revolver.

He snatched up the teapot from the table in front of him and heaved it at Bobby's head in one flashing motion. At the same instant he jumped to the side.

Bobby Hu fired off a wild shot that hit his mother in the shoulder. She gave a choked scream of horror as the blood flower started to bloom on her sleeve.

Tommy was hurling himself across the small room at Bobby now, coming in low to make a more difficult target. Shaken, Bobby fired again and this time the bullet plowed harmlessly into the couch.

He crashed into Bobby below the knees. Bobby hurtled into the outer hallway and the gun went flying from his hand. Tommy slid to a stop on the floor. He reached out to grab Bobby but the slippery young hoodlum rolled frantically out of range.

Both men leaped to their feet at the same time. At close range and without the element of surprise, Bobby Hu had more sense than to stay and try to fight it out with Tommy Lee. He turned and darted up the nearest stairway, running for his life.

Tommy charged up the stairs after him. He pulled out his own automatic and fired off a shot, yelling at Bobby to stop. But Hu turned out of sight onto the next flight of stairs.

Tommy jammed his gun back into the shoulder holster and dashed up the stairs three at a time. He couldn't take the chance on shooting at his only lead to Thunder and

Lightning without a clear aim. A dead Bobby Hu would give no useful information.

The final flight of stairs leading to the roof came into view and the roof door was swinging open. Tommy came through at full speed, knowing that was better than to look around the scene and be a still target for any ambush that awaited.

It proved to be the right decision, as a shot rang out from the left and the bullet breezed by behind his head. Tommy dived to the rooftop. He'd seen the gunflash out of the corner of his eye. Bobby was firing at him from behind a ventilator shaft. There was nothing surprising about a Thunder and Lightning desperado carrying more than one weapon.

Tommy got out his Colt .45 again and fired carefully at the shadows poking out around the iron shaft. Bobby began skittering backwards toward the edge of the roof, keeping the pipe between himself and Tommy. He vaulted over the edge of the roof and disappeared from sight.

Leaping to his feet again, Tommy gave chase. This time he was too close behind to put away his gun in the interests of faster running. He charged full tilt at the roof ledge and didn't slow down as he vaulted over with one hand, down onto what proved to be an adjoining rooftop some eight feet below.

He landed in a crouch and gripping his pistol with both hands he tried another shot at the fleeing Bobby. Bobby kept going and was already leaping onto the next roof.

Tommy took off after him again, charging full tilt across the roof, leaping over the ledge without breaking stride and closing the gap on what proved to be the final rooftop. This was the end of the block.

The line of roofs ended at an alley too wide to jump across even if there had been something handy to grab at on the other side. But Bobby still lucked out. There was a line of fire escapes on this side, leading down to the alley.

Hu began clattering downward along the iron ladders. Tommy laid down on the top bars and fired a shot at the fleeing shadow below, but it was too difficult a target by night. Tommy jumped up and returned to the pursuit.

Bobby got to the bottom fire escape, climbed down the hanging ladder as far as it went and then jumped the rest of the way to the alley. Instead of running out toward the street he was heading back toward the shadowy dead end.

Tommy could hear the mental warning bells going off inside his head as he realized something unexpected was happening. But he was moving too fast to stop the chase. He had reached the bottom fire escape and was jumping over the side to save a few seconds, rather than descending the ladder and dropping the rest of the way.

He bounced on his feet and stood erect, his gun jabbing into the darkness as he tried to figure what was happening. He could hear Bobby's running footsteps and then the sound of a car motor starting up. An auto door slammed shut and then the lights went on at full brightness.

The auto ground forward, revving up momentum as it climbed through the gears. Tommy took aim carefully, standing his ground. He fired directly between the two angry eyes of the headlights.

But the car kept hurtling down upon him. And when he squeezed the trigger again, nothing happened. He was out of bullets in the clip.

But there were three spare clips in custom-tailored pockets sewn inside his jacket. Swiftly he hauled out the empty clip from the butt of the automatic, grabbed a full one from the pocket and slapped it into place. He cocked the gun, pulling back the bolt to get the first bullet into the chamber.

And the gun jammed.

Tommy cursed to himself and jammed the automatic back into the holster. Trying to reload at top speed with headlights blinding you was asking for a clip jam. That was exactly the sort of thing which made him prefer to rely on his superb skills in unarmed martial arts whenever possible.

The catapulting Thunder and Lightning auto was almost on him now, perhaps twenty-five feet away. It took up almost the entire width of the alley and was clearly intent on running him down.

Tommy glanced up at the ladder a few feet above his head. He could almost certainly jump for it and pull himself up to safety. But there he'd be, hanging in the air for vulnerable seconds as a perfect target for the gunners in the car as it went by.

No. Tommy would never flee when he could still attack. He grabbed one of the garbage cans stacked against the wall and threw it into the windshield.

There was a ringing of shattered glass behind the sound of the metal can thunking into the hood. The driver lost control of the steering wheel and swerved directly into the wall toward Tommy.

That was when Tommy knew it was time to jump and grab the fire escape ladder. He lazily swung his feet over the roof of the auto as it slammed into the brick wall and caroomed off.

Despite a smashed headlight and a crumpled front end, the car kept going out of the alley, heading for the open street although cheated of its prey.

Tommy dropped down behind the auto, whirled around and got his gun out again. He yanked out the clip and shoved it back in place once more. This time when he cocked it, the gun fired.

He blasted away at the rear tires and saw the auto start shimmying as he got one tire knocked out. That was all the handicapping he needed and he started to sprint after the crippled car. It couldn't get out of range on only three wheels.

The street was a steep hill and the getaway car had been headed upward when Tommy blew out the tire. As Tommy dashed after it, the driver came up with the devilishly clever ploy of shifting into neutral so the auto suddenly came sliding right back at the pursuer.

Tommy had to dive headlong between two parked autos to save his life. The sliding car smashed over the curb and knocked over a lamp post.

Tommy crawled up onto the sidewalk and poked his gun over the trunk of the nearest parked auto. The looming black shapes of the Thunder and Lightning hoods were spilling out of the car and they were opening up on him with rifles and shotguns.

He knew he couldn't stop them all, but he had enough bullets to keep them from getting him while he was behind cover. A stalemate meant he won. They couldn't wait around to make sure he was finished. They'd have to take off and if he wounded one who couldn't get away then, he'd have his pipeline to the mysteries of the gang.

And then a taxi came innocently around the corner. The cabbie must have been unable to tell where the shots were coming from and so he made a right turn exactly into the battleground.

In a flash, Thunder and Lightning hoods had opened all the taxi doors, clubbed the driver over the head and tossed him into the gutter. They piled into the cab and roared away into the night, leaving Tommy standing there disgustedly.

The next day, Tommy reported back to the war room at Central Tong Headquarters. His first order of business with Lo Sing was to inquire if any progress had been made in tracing the whereabouts of Bobby Hu's current or ex-girlfriend, the go-go dancer turned cocktail waitress whose name was Rosie or Rosalie.

After leaving the scene of last night's shoot-out before the cops could arrive, Tommy phoned in his new information to the tong council and alerted them to send an ambulance for Mrs. Hu. Then he warily headed home for a well-earned rest.

Now Lo Sing said, "I believe we are getting closer to Bobby Hu's lady friend. We should have her traced in a day or so. The last name she was known to be using was Rosalie Carter. She is a cocktail waitress who moves from bar to bar in the North Beach area. Apparently she is one of that pleasurable but troublesome breed of white women who is fascinated by oriental men, so she will not stray far from Chinatown for very long."

"Are she and Hu still lovers?"

"To the best of our present knowledge, yes they are."

Lo Sing led Tommy through the growing file of information that the tongs were assembling about the Thunder and Lightning. This new gang was indeed as formidable as it was mysterious.

It had come very far during the past three years and now apparently had a strong network of contacts between Southeast Asia and the Chinatowns of America. As far as could be seen from the intriguing hints being gathered, the hallmark of Thunder and Lightning was that it concentrated on recruiting only the most loathed and distrusted of outcasts, those who were too wild and bloodthirsty even for the ruthless gangs that operated throughout the Chinese World.

But as far as the leaders of the Thunder and Lightning, or what its ultimate purpose was, still not a clue. Only the continual building up of detail after detail which would eventually reveal the total pattern.

For the next few hours, Tommy went over the collected data with Lo Sing. There were names of suspected members and their known associates, incidents of often startlingly vicious crimes believed to have been committed by the Thunder and Lightning.

"As far as it looks here, most of the members of Thunder and Lightning seem to be either physically ugly people who had difficulty finding acceptance, half-crazed psychopaths and sex perverts, or greedy criminals who double-crossed their own kind," said Tommy.

"Yes," agreed Lo Sing. "And look at the pattern of the crimes we have logged. Notice how there are less of the smaller operations."

"It's as if Thunder and Lightning has now gotten past the phase of raising money to finance their major operation, which is to get into the American heroin business in a big way," said Tommy. "And they've also established themselves as the toughest crowd around, so nobody will mess with them."

Tommy wondered what had become of the Mafia file on Thunder and Lightning, which Lisa Delmonico had promised to messenger to him. According to Lo Sing, the file never arrived. Tommy promptly phoned his office and was informed by Cousin Lotus that no package from the Delmonicos had arrived there either.

When he got Lisa on the phone at the Pacific Heights mansion, she said, "I decided that it would be too risky to send over the file. You'll have to come over and see it."

"Why not?" said Tommy. "I'll be right there."

He drove to the mansion in a nondescript two-year-old Ford that the EWI had left near tong headquarters. He parked inside the gate and once again passed through to the sweeping marble-floored entrance hall.

This time Lisa was waiting for him in a small sitting room on the ground floor. She was posed on an antique plush couch, wearing a lacey long gown. Her black hair was combed tightly back into a short pony-tail held by a comb. Her legs were tucked up under her, only the feet peeking out in soft leather backless heeled slippers.

A folder of thick, brown cardboard was laid out on a coffee table before the couch. Lisa made a languid gesture toward the file, with her cool, pale hand. "Would you like a drink?" she asked.

"A glass of wine would be fine," Tommy said. "Or some coffee." He was already riffling through the papers in the folder as Lisa got up and poured him some transparent-ruby wine from a crystal decanter.

The syndicate had a surprisingly full dossier on Thunder and Lightning, from their own special point of view. Mainly, the information was a log on incidents in which the Mafia had come up against T and L. Surprisingly often, the encounters had ended with the Mafia in full defeat. The effect was often similiar to a Viet Cong operation against the dug-in forces of organized crime's governors.

The earliest reports were dated some two years previous. Mafia representatives had been dispatched to Saigon and Bangkok to make opening explorations into the possibility of starting a Southeast Asia pipeline to the U.S., to support the increasingly difficult Turkey-to-Marseilles route.

In each case the Mafia men were wiped out. They disappeared without a trace. Clearly, there was a strongly organized force in the area with no intention of letting any outsiders gain even the slightest foothold in the dope export trade.

And then about a year ago the attacks had begun on runners and dealers selling heroin to the inner city ghettos of the United States. The Mafia wasn't used to being attacked on its own turf any more. But some mysterious force was obviously making a systematic effort to destroy the Mafia's incredibly lucrative heroin network.

No wonder the mobsters felt they had a problem.

And not one member of the Thunder and Lightning had ever been taken alive by the mob. There were a few more names of suspected members in the file that Tommy knew would be useful to the busy tong researchers.

He took out a pocket notepad and wrote down the dates, places, and names he felt might be most valuable. Then he stood up to leave. His business here was over. "Thanks," he said. "I'll get back on the job." He had no curiosity about how the Mafia summit conference was going, he just didn't care.

"There's something else I've been thinking about," said Lisa, "along with everything else that's going on."

"What's that?"

Nonchalantly, Lisa started to hike up her long white gown, revealing inch after inch of the smooth love-towers of her legs. "I'd like you to lick my pussy," she said. "It would help me relieve my tensions."

"Just like that, huh?" said Tommy. "Some other time that would be an invitingly kinky offer. But right now I've got a few too many other things on my mind. No personal offense intended, but thanks anyway."

"If I were a man and this horny, I'd rape you," Lisa pouted.

"You're not the man in this couple, and that's the basis of our physical relationship," said Tommy.

"We women have our ways," Lisa said as her eyes took on a gleam of mischief. "Even if I can't rape you, I have more subtle means of getting you in the mood."

She reached out for him, calmly opened up his pants and leaned forward to give him head. Her thrusting tongue had the delicately exciting grace of a friendly butterfly.

As Tommy's excitement grew, Lisa was imperceptibly leaning backwards and drawing him toward the couch. Tommy didn't try to fight it and before he fully realized what was happening he was laid out on the couch above Lisa, but with his head poised between her legs.

Oh well, this was certainly better than a coffee break and everybody was entitled to a coffee break. He might as well give this strange, imperious girl what she wanted once more.

He bent down and went into the classic sixty-nine position, thrusting his tongue deeply and actively to see if that was the best way to get her off.

It certainly was, this time. Her muff throbbed up in his face and arched high as he cupped her globed buns from behind. Quickly she drew him into completion and swallowed the discharge. This seemed to be the final signal to shudder brokenly over the orgasm line herself.

One moment she was lying spent and heavy-breathing beside him, then the next moment she had smoothly raised herself up to a sitting position again and in a single movement she swung her legs above Tommy, slipped down her gown and stood up.

She took the Thunder and Lightning folder with her and went to the door. "If that's all you need me for now," she said, "I have to get back to the meeting."

Tommy chuckled. "Far be it from me to hold you up," he said.

"Keep us posted," replied Lisa, very businesslike. She walked out of the room.

Tommy shrugged, straightened out his clothing, and left the mansion. He was beginning to think more and more that the beautiful Lisa Delmonico was a cold-blooded psycho, totally amoral and self-centered. Lucretia Borgia in the old days of Italian blood feuds and power struggles must have been like that.

He made his way back to the teeming streets of Chinatown, driving smoothly and uneventfully. He was trying to think about what the Thunder and Lightning might be expected to do in the next few days—and that was not a very comforting topic.

The T and L gang was clearly not the type of outfit to lay low when things got hot for them. They could be expected to strike back with massive force at any time now. They had already declared war on both the Mafia and the Tongs, as well as on Lo Sing and Tommy himself. The first attack could come at any of these targets.

Tommy climbed the stairs to the tong council room and told Lo Sing, "I have some more pieces for the pattern."

"Good," said the wise sage. He called over several of his chief assistants and soon they were all clucking satisfaction in unison as Tommy read off the key facts he had transcribed in his notebook.

Then when they were done copying down the new information, Lo Sing drew Tommy aside and said, "We also have interesting news. Perhaps the most important revelation yet. But it is something that must be considered deeply and secretly."

So saying, he beckoned over a bald thick-chested man whom Tommy recognized as the semi-retired owner of a small bakery which was now being run by the younger generation of his family.

"Mr. Tsaing here was contacted by his cousin, who wants to lead us to the hide-out of the Thunder and Lightning in exchange for a big reward."

Tommy turned his gaze on the bald baker. Tsaing said, "We had heard something about my cousin Joey joining the Thunder and Lightning, but were not sure. He has gone into hiding for many months. I am ashamed to say my young kinsman is wanted for murder. He killed his best friend in a fight over a girl. Then Joey called me this morning because he knows I was elected to the tong council."

Lo Sing interrupted, "Joey Tsaing told his illustrious cousin that he would lead us to the secret headquarters of the Thunder and Lightning for $50,000 and a safe getaway. He is new to the gang and afraid of their excesses, he does not feel responsibility to join in the bloodbath that seems sure to come."

Tommy nodded and said, "How do we contact Joey?"

"He wants Tommy Lee and Lo Sing to come alone and meet him at the top of Telegraph Hill tonight at three a.m."

"This could be a trap," said Lo Sing. "Yet we have no choice except to check it out."

"No, our only choice is that I must go alone, honorable Lo Sing," said Tommy. "You are far too valuable a leader to our cause to risk in the open."

They argued about that for a while, but eventually the soundness of Tommy's position prevailed. He would go by himself in the dead of night to meet with this supposed informer. It was the only way, trap or no trap.

CHAPTER NINE

Telegraph Hill is probably the best-known viewing point in San Francisco. It is unmistakable from almost anywhere in the city. One of the legendary seven hills and the one surmounted with the oddly nozzle-shaped tower. The Coit Tower had been built by a wealthy widow earlier in the century, in memory of the late Mr. Coit who'd been one of San Francisco's early fire commissioners.

The small parking lot atop Telegraph Hill was never closed off. The hill was not actually a park, the roadway up was a spectacularly winding residential street lined with expensive homes and apartment buildings all the way up to the summit.

This was a particularly apt choice for a public, yet secluded, illicit meeting, Tommy thought. At the late hour of three a.m., the hilltop would probably be deserted. Yet there was always a chance some particularly determined couples might be using it for a lovers' lane or some unusually energetic tourists might be having a look around. Also, you could count on a police car showing up for a look every hour or so, since the place could never be considered shut down completely.

Because of all this, Telegraph Hill had all the advantages of privacy plus the safety of a public place where you couldn't discount the possibility of a witness showing up at any time.

Tommy had driven up Telegraph Hill a few minutes before two a.m. Coming to this sort of meeting at least an hour early and waiting quietly in the background to ensure no ambush was being planned was a normal precaution and something that had been among the earliest lessons Tommy learned at Army Intelligence School in Fort Holabird, Maryland.

Tommy drove up in a deliberately anonymous black Buick. He parked at the far end of the lot and waited. There had been a pair of teenagers necking passionately in a car when he arrived, but they left after ten minutes and then he was alone until a patrol car came up at 2:30. Tommy looked around the shadows, but couldn't spot anything moving.

He settled back to enjoy the spectacular view over the bay, the waterfront, and the twinkling lights of the city. Telegraph Hill was more or less close to directly above Fisherman's Wharf, and the miles of Bay Bridge still had moving auto headlights keeping fairly busy.

At Tommy's side on the front seat was a loaded pump-action shotgun and also a submachine gun with a full clip. No wonder he felt perfectly secure to do a little relaxing meditation as the minutes ticked by in darkness. He didn't want to get his mind all clogged up with unnecessary thinking now. Concentrating on the immediate moment was what counted. And nothing filled the bill for that better than a little zen meditation. In the quiet dead of night, he was perfectly alert while perfectly relaxed, not in danger of either falling asleep or getting needlessly jumpy.

It was exactly thirty seconds before three a.m. when the little Toyota Corolla came burbling up the hill and pulled into the parking area. Tommy nodded in approval, instantly out of his reverie. Nothing could have been more reassuring than for an informant to show up for a meeting in a low-powered little foreign car like this.

It was a move calculated to put Tommy at his ease. Surely nobody would come with intent to ambush and run, in this car. Not unless they had a particularly clever trap in mind. . . .

A small, shadowy figure opened the door of the Corolla and got out from behind the steering wheel. He walked slowly beneath the nearest lamp post and stood there so the light could illuminate his face.

It was Joey Tsaing, all right. Tommy had seen that sullenly furtive face in snapshots shown to him by Tsaing's uncle, the baker, as well as distantly remembering Joey as a fellow street-kid as they were growing up a few years apart in Chinatown.

Tommy got out of his own car and walked over toward the lamp post. But he stopped outside the circle of bright light.

"Lee?" asked Joey, with false bravado.

"That's right," said Tommy. "Come on over here into the shadows. I don't see any point in setting up either of us as perfect targets for any snipers that happen to be in the area."

Joey moved a few hesitant steps toward Tommy. His right hand was thrust deep into the pocket of his loose coat. "Where's Lo Sing?" he demanded. "I want the old man here too."

"Not a chance," said Tommy. "The tong president is too valuable to the entire community to be risked on a set-up like this. I'm here by myself."

"Well, how do I know you won't try to jump me and take me in with your goddamn kung fu?"

Tommy pointed at Joey Tsaing's pocketed right hand. "What are you holding in there, your lucky rabbit's foot? You've got a gun in your hand and I am being careful to stay farther away from you than my punching or kicking range. So you're as safe as you have any right to expect to be, considering the double-cross you're supposedly trying to pull off."

"Lo Sing can talk about money from the tongs' war chest," said Joey. "You can't. That's why he has to be here."

"Where he is, is a crowded all-night coffee shop outside Chinatown, waiting for us with a couple of operatives from my detective agency. There's too many people around for anybody to try something funny. If you convince me up here that you're on the level, I'll take you to him right now and you can work out the money and escape plans."

Joey started to pace around nervously. Tommy had to swing his position around to follow him and when Joey stopped to talk again Tommy had his back toward the Toyota.

This was enough to start making Tommy even more wary. It could have been merely coincidence that Joey had maneuvered him away from sight of the car. On the other hand, this could be the springpoint for a cleverly thought-out ambush.

Tommy watched Joey's face very carefully as Tsaing began to speak again, he was also listening intently for any sounds behind him—particularly for the quiet reopening of a car door or the lowering of a car window.

With great agitation, Joey was saying, "Sure, that's all I need, to get in the car with you. One quick kung fu punch and I'll be a prisoner instead of a guy with valuable information to sell."

"You can ride behind me in the back seat with your gun in the back of my neck," said Tommy. "Or you can follow me in your own wheels. Just don't let me see you in my rearview mirror stopping to make a phone call or trying to use a car radio."

"I don't know," Joey muttered. "You gotta give me an evidence of your good faith. You got any money on you?"

"Only a thousand. That's enough for a starter." Tommy patted his breast pocket. "But I'm going to need some evidence of your good faith before I flash you any green. Tell me something about the Thunder and Lightning that I don't know."

Joey blustered, "If I tell you a piece of what I know, you'll be able to figure out most of the rest. And where's my bread and escape ticket then? Forget it."

"Okay, I'll give you one more chance before I write you off as bad news and split."

"You won't split. You need what I know too much to mess around."

"I'll get into my car and drive to the restaurant where Lo Sing is waiting," said Tommy. "You can follow behind me or not, whatever you like. If you change your mind later, we can try to set up another meet. But if you want that thousand bucks now, let's hear you tell me what you told your uncle about why you want to bust the Thunder and Lightning. And you better make it convincing."

"Who wouldn't want to sell out Thunder and Lightning, they're a bunch of kill-crazy wierdos," said Joey.

"Sure, but all the members seem to like it that way," countered Tommy. "Why are you the one exception?"

"I didn't join up because I was a believer, Lee. I just had no place to go after my buddy Jim got killed in our fight over that bitch," said Joey. "You've seen how the Thunder and Lightning bosses get their boys filled up with all that nonsense mumbo-jumbo about how our desperate courage makes us invincible as a group. It's almost like brainwashing and it eventually gets to guys with nothing else to lose. It would probably get to me too, if I'm cut off from the rest of the world any longer. But I don't owe Thunder and Lightning anything I haven't already paid off and I just want to get far away from them with full pockets . . . before they do brainwash me into being a gung ho kamikaze like the rest of them."

As Joey was talking, Tommy looked into his eyes. And the first thing he noticed as Tsaing rattled on, seemingly unable to stop rapping, was that the renegade seemed to be deliberately willing himself to look anywhere but in Tommy's direction. And then he spotted the last thing he needed to know before acting.

There was a glint of some bright object suddenly reflected in Joey's pupils!

Although Tommy had not heard a sound, he now knew there must be something behind him. He ducked and whirled, caught a glimpse of a shadowy human figure from the corner of his eye and instantly dived to the ground.

Above him, he heard the hissing whoosh of some relatively large object being hurled through the air. And then Joey let out an ear-splitting scream of pain.

Tommy jerked his head over and saw Joey starting to fall over backwards with the handle of a small axe dangling grotesquely from his stomach and blood pouring out of a gaping wound. Joey would be dead before he hit the ground, Tommy knew. The shock would speed the work of the lethal blade.

At the same time, Tommy was drawing his automatic from the shoulder holster and rolling around to face the ambusher who had meant the hurled weapon for him.

But even as he got the Colt .45 free of his clothing the attacking figure was leaping for it in a dark blur of lethal motion. And there was a second hatchet raised high in the attacker's hand.

Tommy squeezed the trigger, knowing even before the shot blasted off that he didn't have the gun properly lined up on the fast-moving figure. The bullet went past into the night and the arm with the hatchet was crashing down upon him.

It was too late to roll out of the way!

Desperately, Tommy reached out with his pistol to parry the death blow. He intercepted the blur of steel with the middle of his gun barrel.

There was a sharp, loud clang of metal on metal. The impact tore the gun out of Tommy's hand and sent it flying over the steep edge of Telegraph hill, scraping his trigger finger raw and sending off one last wild shot.

But he had deflected the death-dealing thrust of the hatchet blade and now he was able to roll backwards for three rapid-fire complete revolutions and then spring to his feet, poised for combat.

And he immediately recognized the single opponent he was facing, although he had never met him before!

It is not too difficult to recognize a man with a nose made out of silver!

He was known now only as Hatchet Wang, a thoroughly evil and treacherous cut-throat whose blood reputation was a familiar tale throughout the Orient. Yet he was universally recognized by all those in a position to know as the last great living exponent of the art of the Chinese assassin hatchet man.

Wang was crouched over the fallen Joey now, pulling out the bloody hatchet he had thrown and thrusting the shaft into his belt after swiftly wiping the blade clean on

Joey's trousers. He gave Tommy a hideously jaunty grin, his silver nose catching glints of the dim moonlight.

Tommy glanced past Wang to his car where the two rifles waited. Forget it. He'd never get by the master hatchet man long enough to bring the guns to bear.

It was to be the barehanded martial arts versus the flashing steel of the Chinese killer hatchet. Tommy stood up straight and made a short bow, which Wang returned. When two acknowledged great fighters met for the first time in mortal combat, there were certain formalities to be followed, formalities that only added more satisfaction to the challenge of the life-and-death struggle that must surely follow.

There was no particular hurry to start this battle. It wasn't fear in either man, more like a savoring of the deliciously tense excitement before a spectacular fight that neither combatant could run away from.

Tommy considered Hatchet Wang, a near-legendary killer that he had heard so much about but never met. Wang must be at least in his mid-fifties by now, but from what Tommy had already seen of him tonight he was as tough, swift, and deadly as ever. Wang had been only a fearsome teenager when he cut his lethal swath through the final great spasm of tong war violence in the early 1930s.

The tale of how he got his silver nose revealed Wang's entire harshly vicious character in toto. It was a tale Tommy had heard on the narrow, teeming streets of a dozen Asian cities since he was a young child.

Wang, whose true given name had already long been replaced by the name of his weapon, committed a loathsome offense against the leaders of his tong and was to be gruesomely punished. Crazed with an overdose of opium, for which he had a fatal weakness, Hatchet Wang had broken into the home of his tong chief, raped the man's daughter and then killed her with his little axe before looting the home of gold and jewels.

Taken alive only after weeks of pursuit and a bloody battle, Wang was sentenced to have his hands chopped off. He came then as close to begging for mercy as a man like him could. He pleaded not for a lighter punishment, but to be killed outright ... slowly and painfully if his captors wished. He preferred agonizing death to walking the earth as a cripple unable to practice his virtuosity with the hatchet.

The strangely warped honor of Wang's about-to-die last request moved the hearts of those seeking rightful vengeance on him in a way that cowardice or defiance never could. "Very well, you may live on with your deadly hatchet arm and your killer soul," said the tong chieftain whose beloved daughter Wang had murdered. "But as long as you live, all the world will see what a monster you truly are."

He ordered Hatchet Wang's nose hacked off as the outlaw humbly thanked him for this mercy.

The noseless face was such a grisly death mask that Wang soon found even the grotesqueness of a silver frame that fitted over the open hole to be an improvement. Through almost four decades of cataclysmic social upheavals in the Far East, the awesome silver-nosed hatchet man became a living legend of ferocious violence for sale to the highest bidder.

He was a feared outcast, often thought to have disappeared from the face of the Earth but eventually popping up somewhere or other in Asia as the deadliest of paid killers. As far as Tommy knew, Wang had never operated in the United States before. And Wang had kept his long-ago oath never to work against his tong or seek revenge on those who disfigured him. It was perhaps the only oath he had ever honored in his long life of violence and shame.

Tommy broke off examining Hatchet Wang and said, "The Thunder and Lightning gang is a natural home for one such as you. I should have expected something like this."

Wang grinned, "Indeed, a small but fatal ambush which you have no hope of escaping. If an entire force of gunmen had come after you here, you would have easily slipped away."

"It is unbecoming to boast, before one's equal," said

Tommy coldly. "We shall see which of us escapes unhurt from what is about to happen, Wang of the Silver nose."

"I meant you no offense," said Wang, he stated this as a fact, not an apology. "I only speak as one who has never been defeated in single combat. To me, this meeting is an honor and a pleasure. I look forward to one of the great struggles of my career." He and Tommy bowed to each other once again.

Tommy stated, "You rode up the hill clinging onto the outside of the car on the passenger side so I couldn't see you."

"Of course. And then when your back was to the little car I came around silently and moved up behind you. I do not believe you heard me coming, it must have been the facial expression of my poor departed comrade Tsaing that warned you."

"That, and the glint of light on metal reflected in his eye. I had thought first it must be a weapon, but now I imagine it was your nose."

Wang took no offense. It was an interesting new point of information for him. "Yes, I usually blacken the silver for night hunting. But I expected the silence of my approach behind you to be enough this time. Truly you will be a most formidable opponent. Shall we begin?"

"One moment more, if you please," said Tommy. "I would like to know if you are one of the actual leaders of Thunder and Lightning."

"Alas, no, my old wits would not be equal to such a task," said Wang. "I merely practice my long-held profession in the service of those who appreciate it perhaps more than any others in the world possibly could."

"I thank you," said Tommy. "In that case it will not be necessary for me to attempt to take you alive at all costs."

"I would not want you to fight me under that mistaken belief," Wang said. And they both knew now that the talk was over.

Tommy and Wang bowed to each other one final time and began their fight to the death. Both realized that from here on in, the formal politeness was over and now even the most unfair tactics would be used whenever possible.

CHAPTER TEN

It would have to take a little while for the tempo of the fight to build up. Each man had to get some idea of the style of moves the other had.

But of course any real opening would have meant the split-second destruction of the careless combatant.

Tommy and Wang circled warily around each other, each searching for an opportunity to test the speed of his attack. Theoretically, Wang's razor-sharp hatchets which could be swung or accurately thrown, should have given him the clear advantage over an unarmed man.

But in the case of a grand master of the martial arts like Tommy Lee, each of his bare hands and shod feet were a lightning-fast and deadly weapon. And both men understood this full well. On the other hand, Wang's predominant reliance on the instantly lethal blade of his small axe somewhat limited the variety of his movements and left much of his body vulnerable once he had committed himself to an attack position.

So despite Tommy's lack of any weapons, both he and Wang clearly recognized that this was a near-even match.

Normally, Tommy would have soon feinted a strong attack at any opponent, an attack that he could have followed through with deadly force instantly if the fake-out worked. But this wouldn't do with a speedy and experienced hatchet man like Wang. Tommy couldn't take the chance of leaving himself vulnerable to even the slightest touch of the fierce blade, for even a light slash of the razor edge would do him severe damage.

Thus, Tommy was perfectly ready to circle around and make only basic hand feints for hours, if that's what it took to wear down the older Wang. But almost as if Wang knew what his responsibility was toward heating up the action, he made his first charge.

Bellowing an awesome shout like an enraged water buffalo, Wang rushed at Tommy head-on, slashing his hatchet through the air in a blinding-fast pattern as he came. The hatchet moved up, down and sideways in seemingly random sequences and the darting blade was a sight to deeply frighten even the most brave of men . . . if the man being attacked didn't know how to handle it.

Tommy simply stepped to the left, toward the weaker side of the right-handed thrust. And as Wang rushed past him, trying to halt the hatchet charge and come around again, Tommy lashed out a mighty kick with his right leg.

The kick would have been more than enough to cave in Wang's ribs if it had landed on target. But with incredible adeptness, Wang managed to pivot and swerve just enough so that the kick caught on his hipbone, producing no more than a bruise.

Backhanded, Wang snaked a hatchet chop at Tommy's still-extended leg. Tommy barely had time enough to duck and roll, letting the hatchet swipe above his crouched body.

He reached up and slammed a knife-hand karate punch at the hatchet arm, but only grazed it. He and Wang both stepped quickly back, ready to catch their breaths before the next lightning-fast onslaught.

There was no need to do any more formal bowing. But almost at the same instant, the two men inclined their heads respectfully to each other. It was a mutual gesture of admiration for the opponent's unexpectedly superb skills, a recognition that here and now had been found the ultimate challenge for their martial arts capabilities.

And then Wang charged again, this time leaving out the enraged buffalo roar. He had the hatchet up over his head and then as he thrusted down with what seemed like irresistible force, he suddenly looped the stroke completely around and came smashing upwards with the hatchet at Tommy's groin.

This time, Tommy completely reversed his previous

strategy of counterattack. He darted in at Wang from the right side, coming in close, inside the arc of the hatchet. With both hands he grabbed the hatchet arm near the elbow.

He couldn't take a chance of staying close in to Wang for long, not while the man had a second axe in his belt within reach of his free arm. Tommy stepped forward in the direction of Wang's momentum and flipped the peerless hatchet man over his shoulder in a classic judo-style throw.

But Wang was too much the experienced pro to let this tactic immobilize him for more than an instant after he landed. He absorbed the impact of falling with his feet and his buttocks, coming up with his hatchet already poised to strike upwards. And he merely pulled his head back out of the way of the kick Tommy launched at him.

Once again, Tommy had all he could do to hurl himself aside as the riposte stroke of the hatchet swiped at his leg.

They backed apart for a second time. Wang indulged himself by looking around briefly toward the uppermost apartment buildings along the hilltop roadway. Tommy jerked his head at him. This time it wasn't a bow, it was a nod.

As might have been expected, there were lights on in the windows and outlined human shapes peering out to try to see what was going on in the shadows of the parking area that had caused those screams or shouts. It now had to be only a matter of minutes before the police car someone must have already summoned came sirening up.

And Tommy as well as Wang had reasons not to want the fight to still be going on then the cops arrived. The duo went back into their wary attack shuffle.

And this time Tommy did not wait for Wang to come at him. He sprang forward and launched himself off his feet in an awesome two-legged bucket kick.

Wang swung forward with the hatchet to slice Tommy's legs off in midair.

But suddenly Tommy had changed his bullet-fast trajectory. He sat up in mid-air and switched directions, almost like some horrendously difficult piece of ballet dancing. Almost faster than the eye could follow, he had landed on his feet close behind Wang's back. And his knife-edge karate swipe caught Wang's right arm just where it joined the shoulder.

The stunning force of the blow momentarily paralyzed Wang's arm and the hatchet clattered to the pavement.

Yet before Tommy could follow up his new advantage, Wang struck back in a totally unexpected manner. He snatched the second hatchet from his belt and whirled out of Tommy's punching range at the same time as he swept a rapid backhand blow with the hatchet in his left fist.

Tommy barely got out of the way in time. "So you're ambidextrous," he said, catching his breath. "That's your secret."

"It's one of my secrets," corrected Wang. "And I'm not quite as good with my left hand, I have to admit. Just a hair slower. But it's fast enough to finish you off now."

"Maybe if I knock out both your hands, you can shake off your silver nose and shove the hatchet handle into the hole," suggested Tommy.

Furious, Wang reared back and threw the hatchet at Tommy's heart. Tommy hadn't expected Wang to try a throw with his left hand. Caught offguard, he could only hurl himself backwards to escape the missile.

And the point of the hatchet blade actually grazed his forehead as it went by, leaving a light surface cut that bled slowly and thickly in a way that meant it would soon clot up. If the hatchet had cut him a few millimeters deeper, enough blood would no doubt be pouring down his forehead to swiftly blind him.

As it was, Tommy rolled to his feet and saw Wang snatching up the first hatchet he'd dropped. Wang held it in his right hand and briefly massaged the bicep with his left. He took a few experimental swipes with the right arm and nodded to himself in approval.

Then he came stalking forward. The hatchet was held out in his right hand. He moved directly, with nothing tricky about his approach. He kept on advancing until he got close enough so that Tommy had to do something.

What Tommy did was to try to step in around behind

him again and land punches with both arms on Wang's neck and spine while he kicked out at the man's legs.

And what Wang did was to toss the hatchet from the right hand into his left and come at Tommy from a totally unexpected angle. He got within an inch of gashing open Tommy's intestines. The solid kick that Tommy put into Wang's hard thigh hardly compensated for such a close call.

Suddenly there was something new. An auto came around the final bend of the hill and rolled into the parking area.

Both combatants froze for an instant of surprise. Tommy quickly registered that this wasn't any police car, just a pair of late-night lovebirds in a banged-up Pinto out for a bit of necking-with-a-view.

The car was coming almost directly at Tommy. He whirled and ran to meet it. With only one hatchet in Wang's possession right now, Tommy doubted Wang would try a throw at his back. He ran crouched over anyway.

As he'd already seen, the driver's window was open. Tommy ran up, shoved the startled teenage driver aside and grabbed the steering wheel. Without letting go of the wheel, he jumped off the ground and got his torso on the roof of the little car. His legs dangled over the side and he aimed the Pinto directly at Wang.

He'd hoped the driver would be too confused to step on the brake before Tommy ran Wang down. But a lack of pressure applied to the gas pedal had the same effect of screwing up Tommy's improvised plan. Wang easily stepped aside as the car rolled slowly by him.

But meanwhile Tommy had swung one foot onto the auto's hood, stepped up onto the roof and jumped off the other side onto Wang. He kicked Wang's hatchet arm aside and got the other foot into Wang's chest as he slammed down.

Wang somehow managed to keep hold on his hatchet as he fell. Tommy had to scramble off the struggling man before he could bring the blade around again.

And then the sirens announced that a police car was

rocketing up Telegraph Hill. Wang jumped up and turned to run. He plunged over the short brick wall that circled the hilltop and started crashing down the steep, dark undergrowth.

With no hesitation, Tommy took off after him.

This side of the high hill, which faced the bay, had no buildings on it. The hillside was far too steep, with no gentle slopes. Tommy scrambled down after the fleeing shape of Wang the hatchet man.

Tommy could go rather rapidly, if he ignored the stinging scratches of the thorny vines and sharp rocks that lined the dark hillside. He let his momentum carry him faster and faster. At some parts of the hillside he could just keep jumping, letting his heels dig into the terrain and slide him from purchase to purchase. Yet at more rugged and perpendicular sections of the hill he had to grasp with his hands in a semi-climbing position to make continuing the descent possible.

Up above him, he could see the beams of police flashlights stabbing down in his direction. But there were already too many spurs and outcroppings of rock he had passed to allow the lights to find him. Tommy was not too concerned that the cops could trace him to the action above. The Buick he'd arrived in was rented with false identification by one of his East-West Investigations operatives. The weapons he'd left behind were untraceable and wiped free of fingerprints. Tommy had worn a pair of light and flexible driving gloves all evening up to the point when he and Wang started their formal combat stalking.

As a matter of fact, Tommy wished he had the gloves out of his pocket and was wearing them again right now, to protect his hands from the scrapes of the rocks and shrubbery.

He could see he was closing the gap on Wang. This wasn't too surprising, considering his great age advantage on the still-ferocious hatchet killer. Tommy was willing to try an attack on Wang right here on the steep hillside. He felt that the uneven footing and tricky vision would work far more to his advantage than to his opponent's.

He pushed on even more quickly, with barely controlled recklessness. For a moment, he couldn't help chuckling playfully to himself at the confusion that must be going on above. The police would find a dead Chinese and two abandoned cars. He was sure that the couple in the Pinto would be too confused by the speed and surprise of what had happened to give any helpfully accurate descriptions of him to the police. If they remembered any details, it would be of the Chinese with the small axe and the silver nose.

And then below, Tommy heard Wang stumble and slide down a pebble-strewn slope, yelping in pain. Wang stopped and laid there with the side of his head pressed into the hillside. His legs were sprawled out in an awkward position. He wasn't moving at all.

Tommy approached cautiously. It had been a very convincing fall. But he had already been given ample display how agile and tricky Wang was. The man had nothing to lose by playing possum on the hillside to lure Tommy into hatchet range.

Tommy angled his descent off to one side, so he'd be less vulnerable as he approached Wang. Only Wang's left hand was in view, and the fist was empty. His right hand was hidden beneath his still body and could well be gripping the hatchet, poised to strike. Tommy would come in from the left.

Then his feet kicked loose a miniature barrage of small rocks and he halted. He had a better idea. Tommy grinned broadly as he picked up a hefty piece of stone he could barely stretch his fingers around.

He hauled back and bounced the rock off Wang's head. A trickle of blood started running out of Wang's graying hair and over his ear. Tommy hefted a second rock and tossed it at Wang, this time it struck on the back with a loud and painful-sounding thud. Wang still hadn't moved, except to bounce from the impact of each blow.

But Tommy wanted to get in a few more solid head shots before he decided Wang was really immobilized. He found a longish, sharp-pointed rock and raised himself up onto his knees for more accuracy in throwing.

His body was outlined in the moonlight. And that was

when Wang sprang up and charged at him with his hatchet blade up. Apparently Wang just couldn't take it any more to lie there in fake defenselessness as the rocks thudded dangerously into his skull.

Tommy hurled the stone in his hand and it bounced off Wang's chest, but Wang kept coming in a near-silence that was even more threatening than his earlier shouting had been. Tommy easily scrambled upwards, out of range. Wang never even bothered to try a strike of his hatchet.

It wasn't that Tommy was afraid to face Wang on the hillside, but he saw no reason to stand before a head-on attack of the hatchet on such treacherous ground. If he did fight with Wang on the hill, it would be from above, where Wang's upward hatchet strokes could be far more easily deflected.

But Wang could see what a disadvantage Tommy's choice of position would leave him in. And he wasn't having any part of it. He ignored his pursuer and struck off down the remainder of the hillside, head-first like a lizard.

This mode of descent kept him moving far faster than before. It took Tommy by surprise for a moment, and then he spent another moment observing how Wang was doing his lizard-climb, filing the information into his mind for future use.

By the time Tommy went after him, he had no chance of catching Wang on the hillside. He moved down the rest of Telegraph Hill as fast as he could, allowing no further distractions. This was no time for him to start experimenting with the lizard climb.

He got to the base of the hill just in time to see Wang dashing around the corner of the nearest street.

Tommy took off in hot pursuit. He didn't really think Wang was fleeing from him out of fear. The wily hatchet man just wanted to be able to choose his own ground before they continued fighting. He only had one of his weapons left and so he probably couldn't take a chance on throwing the hatchet unless he had a sure shot. Rather than face Tommy for another series of stand-offs he would probably prefer to try to sneak up on him again.

Tommy turned the corner after Wang, running down the center of the gutter so that he had plenty of open space around him on all sides. He had no intention of leaving himself within range of an arm with a hatchet thrusting out of the shadows.

The street was deserted. Wang couldn't possibly have reached the far end of the block in the few seconds he had been out of Tommy's sight. Therefore he must have found a suitable ambush place and was lying in wait nearby.

Tommy dropped to a crouch behind a parked auto and considered his best strategy. The first rays of dawn were lighting up this long night and Tommy knew he had time on his side. The last minutes of darkness would be far more valuable to Wang.

He scanned the seemingly empty block. This was a typical San Francisco residential street, lined with Victorian-style townhouses and sloping downward in a slight incline. Tommy knew that a few blocks away was the start of the warehouse district that circled the waterfront.

Patiently, Tommy scanned both sides of the street again, trying to spot anything that looked out of place. And then, on the sidewalk ahead of him he heard the metallic clink of a garbage can being jostled.

Tommy stood up behind the car. He peered in the direction of the sound but couldn't see any sign of Wang. The noise could have been made by an alley cat, or perhaps by something tossed by Wang to decoy him.

But Tommy knew he had to check it out. He moved carefully onto the sidewalk. This area of the block had a row of apartment buildings with recessed outer hallways three steps up from the pavement. Wang was not in any of the hallways, as far as Tommy could see.

A wrought iron fence cut off the sidewalk here. These buildings had basement apartments reached with stairs down from the street. The garbage cans were also stored below street level.

Moving quietly and carefully, Tommy looked over the iron-spiked fence and saw nothing in the cans below. Behind him, he only just barely heard the sound of a soft thud.

He whirled around and there was Wang, almost on him with his deadly hatchet at shoulder height. Wang was leaping down the entry stairs from the nearest hallway.

In a flash, Tommy realized how cleverly Wang had tricked him. The hatchet man must have used his hands and feet to propel himself up the opposing walls of the narrow hallway. There Wang held himself in place against the ceiling by the same human-fly method. He was hidden from sight by a decorative archway that blocked off the real hallway ceiling from view of the street.

And a man strong and limber enough to make that climb would also be able to peer under the archway with one eye to keep track of Tommy's progress, and to flick a coin among the garbage cans while Tommy's back was turned in order to lure him closer.

But it was going to require more than explanations and understanding to keep Tommy alive. The hatchet was already slashing out at him.

Tommy was not in a good position to parry Wang's hatchet arm. Instead he dived forward and tucked himself into a ball, rolling forward with the force of his impetus and slamming right into Wang's legs just below the knee. Tommy's body was too low for the hatchet blow to get at it.

Wang went shooting frontward, over Tommy's balled body. He struck the sidewalk with the side of his head.

Tommy came out of his ball position on his hands and knees and jumped up to a kung fu fighting stance.

Wang had rolled on his side and was still sitting on the pavement. In a flash, but too late, Tommy realized what was about to happen. Wang had his arm cocked in throwing position to launch the hatchet into Tommy's guts at easy point-blank range.

Tommy slid back but the waist-high iron fence was right behind him. He had no place to escape to.

CHAPTER ELEVEN

Wang cackled in triumph and threw the hatchet.

But Tommy dove across the top of the iron-bar fence and rolled off to the other side.

He had no time to choose his landing spot and crashed headlong onto a line of garbage cans and paper bags filled with discarded liquor bottles. His ankle twisted under him as he slid off the cans onto the concrete floor of the alley.

The hatchet had bounced off the apartment bricks directly behind where Tommy had been standing an instant before. It clattered down and landed in the basement alley within easy reach of Tommy.

He grabbed the handle and pulled himself erect with his other hand on the garbage cans. Wang peered down over the fence railing at him, his face impassive.

Tommy brandished the hatchet at its owner. "Stay where you are, silver-nose," he said. "I'll give you back something that belongs to you."

He started to climb up the stairs to the street but his twisted ankle gave him a stab of pain and he fell forward. After a moment's pause he continued his upward progress by crawling.

Wang watched him briefly and then raised his empty fist in the traditional Chinese warrior salute. "I thank you, Tommy Lee," he said. "You have undoubtedly given me the greatest fight I ever had. Until the next time we meet . . ." He turned and ran off, his footsteps pattering into silence.

Wang knew better than to face even a hobbled Tommy Lee in a fight minus hatchets.

By the time Tommy got up to sidewalk level and

shoved open the fence gate he could hear chattering from behind windows in the nearby buildings. For the second time tonight the noise of his struggles had awakened neighboring citizens and the arrival of summoned police would be a swift matter.

His ankle felt sprained, rather than broken. But he couldn't walk fast enough to get back to Chinatown on foot with police searching for him. There was only one thing to do.

He limped to the nearest auto and smashed in the side window with Wang's hatchet. He crawled into the driver's seat, got his set of lock picks out of a pocket and in little over thirty seconds had started the ignition and roared off down the street.

He drove back to tong headquarters without any police cars coming across him. He limped inside the building and instructed one of the door guards to leave the stolen car someplace just outside Chinatown. "If you can find the owner's phone number from the name on his registration, call and tell him where to find the car," said Tommy. He handed the guard a hundred-dollar bill from his wallet. "Leave this in the glove compartment," he said.

Lo Sing had returned to central tong headquarters when Tommy didn't show up at their prearranged coffeehouse meeting place within an hour of the appointment. He was waiting anxiously for some news of Tommy's safe arrival.

"Your leg!" he exclaimed as Tommy stumbled wearily into the conference room.

"It's nothing, just a sprain. Our Chinatown healers can make it good as new in just a few hours." He quickly ran down for the tong leader what had taken place on Telegraph Hill and the clever trap he had barely managed to avoid.

"So Hatchet Wang of the silver nose has joined the Thunder and Lightning as an ordinary gang soldier," mused Lo Sing when Tommy was finished. "And for the first time he is operating in North America. Thunder and Lightning must be even more formidable than we had imagined, if they can command the loyalty of a man like Hatchet Wang."

There was nothing more to be done just then except for adding a few more cards of information to the fast-growing tong file system that was outlining the dimensions of the mysterious international band of criminals.

Tommy commandeered a comfortable office couch to get himself some sleep. He was too exhausted from his ordeal to go home. He left word that he had to be awakened in mid-afternoon and set a few appointments before falling asleep.

On being awakened, a little over eight hours later, Tommy was immediately driven a short distance across town to the Japanese district. Part of the gleaming Japanese Trade Center complex was occupied by an authentic Japanese bath facility where Shiatsu Massages were available.

Tommy gratefully began loosening his muscles in the series of hot and cold bathing pools and showers prescribed by the age-old bathing ritual. His leg was already feeling much better by the time he went into the next room and laid down on the massage table.

A little old lady spent the next forty minutes poking his body with her rock-solid extended fingers. Shiatsu was Japan's adaptation of the ancient Chinese art of acupuncture, it worked directly on the nerve centers rather than the muscles. And it had almost magical effectiveness in relieving soreness and aches.

Tommy felt full of alertness and revived energy as he left the baths. A change of clothing had been brought to him from his apartment and his ankle only throbbed slightly as he was chauffered back to the central tong building.

There in a small office was waiting one of the tong councilmen who also happened to be Chinatown's most adept herbalist. He clucked briefly over the condition of Tommy's sprained ankle ligaments, unable to find in his lifetime of habits the open-mindedness to approve of Tommy seeking out "foreign" Japanese treatment as well as his own.

The herbalist applied a series of hot cloths to Tommy's ankle, each cloth was soaked in a different medicinal preparation. Meanwhile a brewing pot of hot water had been readied and the herbalist had Tommy drink three different cups of strange tea. He brusquely ordered Tommy to rest as much as possible for the next twenty-four hours and keep the foot raised as much as possible.

But Tommy had only a few minutes of sitting back on the couch with his legs spread out before him when Lo Sing came in, looking worried.

"I hate to disturb you during your recovery," said the tong chairman. "But the fact is that the Mafia leaders have been demanding that you come and see them immediately. They began phoning for you at noon and their calls have gotten increasingly agitated in tone."

"Of course, I'm ready to meet with them," said Tommy. "But really, most wise Lo Sing, you should have told me about this as soon as I awoke."

"Your health is far more important to me than the whims of drug merchants," said Lo Sing firmly.

Tommy smiled and applied the final phase of treatment to his weakened ankle, winding an elasticized athletic bandage around it for support. When he got up from the couch, only a slight stiffness in his gait betrayed the injury he had suffered at sunrise. He would be able to move as quickly as he needed to in any fight that came up now.

There was an overwhelming atmosphere of on-edge jumpiness among the guards at the rented Mafia mansion when Tommy got there this time. They all seemed to be looking around over their shoulders every few seconds.

Under heavily armed escort, Tommy was brought into the richly paneled library den where the international Mafia bosses council was meeting. Bartlett Delmonico stood warily behind a scrolled antique table at the end of the room, with his young wife Lisa sitting regally by his side.

The assembly of syndicate capos stared at Tommy warily. Delmonico opened by saying, "You wouldn't be trying a double-cross on us now, would you, Mr. Lee?"

"Not hardly," shot back Tommy. "And I've taken too many lumps lately while trying to live up to my side of the agreement to have very much patience with this kind of crap! What's going on? What the hell is bugging you?"

"All right, I'll fill you in if you'll just be patient a moment. First tell us what your tongs have accomplished so far, please."

"Okay. I have to admit that we still don't have our key breakthrough to the leadership and hideout of the Thunder and Lightning yet. But there have already been a couple of close shots, and the way our information core is growing, I'm ready to guarantee we'll be able to strike back soon. It's only a matter of time."

"How much time? That's exactly what's so important to us at this moment."

"A week or maybe two. No more than that, at the rate we're going. An outfit the size of Thunder and Lightning can't help leaving traces behind. And we're steadily picking up more and more of those traces."

Delmonico sighed deeply and the rest of the Mafia council looked unhappy. "Unfortunately, that isn't good enough to meet our present needs," he told Tommy. "Isn't there any way you could be ready to counterattack the Thunder and Lightning leaders in, say, forty-eight hours."

"Sure, if we're lucky and get a big enough breakthrough, everything else will fall into place," countered Tommy. "But you know as well as I do you can't count on a lucky break when you're scheduling something like this."

One of the gristly old men sitting off to the side shouted, "That's it then. We gotta split. Can't afford another Appalachia."

Delmonico held up his hand commandingly as Lisa jumped up beside him. It was Lisa who spoke first, saying coldly, "This is a serious matter for full council vote. Since when do capos debate and vote in front of outsiders." She glared around the room.

Delmonico nodded agreement. He told Tommy, "You seem to be acting upfront with us and you've got a right to know what's happening." He gestured at Tommy to take a seat.

When Tommy had made himself comfortable, Delmonico commenced, "We had another contact from the Thunder and Lightning gang this morning. It was by phone and our electronics boys got a trace on it. A squad was rushed out to the location and when they got there they found a tape recorder keeping open the circuits of a pay phone. They also found that the phone booth was booby-trapped and we lost four good, dependable soldiers in the explosion. But the message we got was that the $200,000 extortion demand was off. Now they want us out of town and not making any waves as they start opening up more of the Asia heroin connection. I guess the earlier money demand was just a test to see how far they could push us around."

"What's supposed to happen if you don't pack in this conference?" Tommy wanted to know.

"They'll storm the mansion and wipe us out within forty-eight hours. That's the new ultimatum."

Tommy shrugged, "You believe they can beat you here with an all-out attack right in the middle of a city?"

"Our troops could stand them off, I believe," replied Delmonico. "But that's not the point. Our real danger here is being exposed to the local authorities if a fight breaks out. We might well be liable to imprisonment on conspiracy charges. At the very least, we'd be dragged before San Francisco grand juries, embarrassed in front of our families and legit associates, and be used as an excuse to kick off another round of national Mafia conspiracy investigations. We can't afford word leaking out that we're meeting here, in other words."

"So end the conference and get out of town," said Tommy. "I don't see how much you can expect to accomplish now anyway, with Thunder and Lightning still at full strength and able to keep on with their own plans for the heroin traffic."

"That's all true enough," said Delmonico. "What we've been doing here the last two days is only contingency planning, deciding how to best handle the situation after you and your tongs get rid of Thunder and Lightning for us. You see, we're assuming you're going to succeed."

"That's very flattering," said Tommy. "So what's your problem about breaking up the meeting?"

"There's two problems and they ought to be obvious," snapped Lisa. More and more she was revealing herself as one of the top mob leaders, on a level with any of the men in the room except Bartlett Delmonico. "Aside from the ill-effects of showing weakness by giving in to the orders of this crazy rabble, the whole thing could be a trap designed to lure us out into ambush. Look what happened to the team we sent out to check the traced phone call!"

Delmonico cut in, "We're a lot safer here than we'd be anywhere else in San Francisco right now. As you know, this place has been made into a fortress and it would be nearly impossible to break through. If we split up and try to make it to our private jets at the airport, we'll be a hell of a lot easier to pick off."

Tommy nodded, understanding fully at last. "You don't need me to tell you it's a tough decision. All I can promise you is we'll keep doing our best to track down the Thunder and Lightning. And I'd suggest that you at least have some plans ready to make a fast getaway to the airport if you decide that's what you want to do."

"That's exactly one of the things we've had under discussion," said Lisa. "We feel that limousines would be too vulnerable in the street right now. Do you know where we could rent a fleet of several armored cars to stand by for evacuation? You know, the kind of truck that delivers money between banks."

"Why not?" said Tommy. "I can find you the phone numbers of the best companies to try."

"Fine, let's do that now on your way out."

Tommy no longer had any reason to be surprised that Lisa found a reason to leave a mansion conference along with him. He looked around the room and saw no sign that anybody disapproved of Lisa's obvious tactic, including the husband-disguised-as-father, Bartlett Delmonico. Seemingly on this social level, matters of sexual loyalty were considered of minor importance next to the unified policies of power.

The pair entered the corridor together. As for Tommy himself, he had no objection to Lisa's favorite brand of intensive recreation right now. He could use a little relaxation after all he'd been through last night. And he saw no reason to be uncomfortable in a crowded cubicle with their positions improvised.

"As long as I'm here, we might as well check around the upstairs windows and see if there's any suspicious new developments in the street. If Thunder and Lightning is really planning an assault, they've probably got a pretty effective trick or two in mind."

"All right," said Lisa. "That's a good idea. We'll get the armored car company numbers afterwards." She led him up the grand staircase.

Swiftly, they went through the charade of entering several of the bedrooms where the visiting mobsters had stored their gear. Tommy peered around through the windows at nearby rooftops, unable to see anything suspicious. Actually it had already gotten dark enough so that there were a number of shadowed areas he couldn't examine clearly enough to tell if there were any snipers hidden there.

The fourth room they entered was larger and classier than the others. Even without the feminine makeup items on the dressing table Tommy would have known this was Lisa's bedroom. He clicked the lock shut behind them and started kissing Lisa roughly while peeling her out of her sweater and trouser suit.

The number they were falling into this time was making love in total silence. It was their busy hands and kisses that were doing all the communication necessary. There was only one dim bedside lamp on as they finished stripping each other and fell onto Lisa's bed, breathing heavily and explosively.

The bed had a big pile of pillowed bolsters at the head and Lisa propped herself up against it so that she was sitting nearly erect and above Tommy, although Tommy was actually over her with his body.

They coupled without requiring a great deal of preparatory heating up and soon were rocking the bed with their passionate lovemaking. Tommy found himself so satisfied by the tigerish excitement with which Lisa was rocking him that he had unusual difficulty in holding back his climax.

He was glad that Lisa quickly reached her own peak and he gratefully joined her in the shuddering orgasm.

"That was great," said the girl, her breasts heaving. "I feel like I'm on fire. As a matter of fact, I can almost smell the flames and hear them crackling."

"That's odd," said Tommy. "So can I."

He looked up through the window. And farther on down along the mansion rooftop, real flames were starting to burn redly downward along the building.

CHAPTER TWELVE

The mansion was on fire, with real and fiercely hot flames licking down from the rooftop.

Tommy leaped out of bed and grabbed for his clothes, tossing a handful of Lisa's garments at his just-finished sex partner.

"Come on, get dressed," he ordered. "Fast! Whatever we have to do about this, we're going to look pretty stupid running around in the nude."

They both clothed themselves with silent rapidity. As Tommy was finishing fastening his pants, he heard the familiar cry of a fire engine siren howling down the street and coming up fast. "Hell, that's pretty fast for a fire department response," he said. "Unless they're sending them by radio these days."

He hopped to the window and saw the full-size San Francisco fire engine racing up to the mansion gate. The gate guards below seemed undecided about whether to unlock the metal bars without specific orders.

But the fire engine didn't even slow down as it turned hard left onto the driveway. It crashed right through the gate, scattering the iron bars like toothpicks with its terrific massiveness and power.

Only one of the guards managed to scramble out of the way in time. The others were run down and crushed. The fire engine plunged straight across the lawn to the front steps.

It screeched to a halt and uniformed firemen leaped off the engine. They reached under their rubber coats and whipped out U.S. Army submachine guns of various configurations.

As the mansion guards poured out the front door and around the sides of the house, the phony firemen opened up and blasted them away in an eerie near-silence. Their weapons had silencers, to avoid alerting the neighborhood that this was more than an ordinary fire for as long as possible.

The Mafia defenders got off few shots before they fell. Their bullets bounced harmlessly off the the firemen's loose rubber coats and metal helmets. The attackers obviously had on bulletproof armor underneath.

Two firemen uncoiled a few lengths of the fire engine hose and blasted off a jetstream of water that collapsed every front window on the ground floor as well as clearing a pathway beyond the open front doors. The firemen dashed for the mansion as soon as the water was shut off again.

Tommy said, "The Thunder and Lightning sure do know how to get it on. Ripping off a fire engine is too much."

Lisa still wasn't out of her confused shock. "But how did they set the fire without us spotting it up here?" she sputtered.

"Incendiary shell of some kind. They shot it out of either a mortar or a rocket launcher. An easy shot and they could have done it from blocks away. These boys don't seem to have any shortage of military weapons from Vietnam."

"We didn't hear any shell hit the roof," insisted Lisa.

"We were distracted for a few minutes," explained Tommy, "hitting the old bed pretty good ourselves."

And then they both heard the choppy whirr of the big helicopter close overhead.

Momentarily frozen in surprise, they could follow the sound of the rotors coming in fast from behind the mansion, hovering directly over the gabled roof for no more than fifteen seconds and then roaring off into the distance again.

But while the copter was hovering over the gabled rooftop, there was also the clear thumping sound of perhaps a dozen pairs of combat boots jumping onto the roof.

Footsteps fanned out over the roof surface. One set of footsteps came directly over the bedroom where Lisa and Tommy waited. There was a short scraping sound in the roof tiles above and in a moment a black-clad shape dropped alongside the window on a rope.

The black-clad figure had an automatic rifle slung under one arm. He kicked in the window and leaped into the bedroom, not yet aware there were two people inside.

As broken glass stopped tinkling, Tommy darted to the bed and tossed one of the fluffy pillows at the invader. Catching only a glimpse of what was being thrown at him, the figure in black cut loose with his silencered submachine gun and loosed a sudden snowstorm of feathers.

Tommy used this instant cloud as cover and dived low across the floor, tackling the gunman and bringing him down. He reached upward for the throat, holding down the gun with his other hand as he snapped the man's neck.

He heard Lisa's voice behind him saying, "Very quick indeed. I liked that."

When he turned, she was peering out from behind the bed. She stood up and only then could Tommy see that Lisa was cradling a pump-action shotgun in her arms.

"You keep that under your bed?" he asked incredulously.

"Always."

They could hear heavy footsteps, breaking windows, and jumping bodies all along the upper-floor rooms now. Tommy said, "Can you really use that mother?"

"Watch me," she said.

"You're on," Tommy said.

He walked rapidly to the door, kicked it open, and barely extending his rifle barrel into the hallway he shot out all the ceiling lights along the corridor in one swift burst. Then he dropped to the floor and crawled into the hallway.

He could smell the perfume of Lisa Delmonico as she

crawled out alongside him. He whispered, "Cover the other direction."

He heard some rustling shadows up ahead and blasted out. There was a sound of screams and bodies falling. A door from a nearby bedroom opened, letting in a slightly brighter band of light from the street lamps beyond the windows.

A shadow was outlined coming through the open door and Tommy shot it down. Behind him he heard Lisa's shotgun scattering clouds of death pellets and shouts of pain from down the corridor.

Bullets chewed through the darkness above him and he fired back until there were no more answering shots. Footsteps were running up behind him, only to be halted by another blast of Lisa's shotgun.

The pair lay silently for a half minute. There were no other sounds in the corridor, not even any heavy breathing. Lisa whispered, "Could we really have gotten them all?"

Tommy sighed quietly. "I guess there's only one way to find out for sure. Get ready."

Tommy crawled backwards in the darkness, returning to Lisa's bedroom. He tugged at the girl's arm to pull her back alongside him. When they were both crouched against the wall by the doorway, Tommy reached up and flicked on the main bedroom light switch.

The hallway was lined with nine or ten bleeding, black-clad bodies of young Chinese men. Another black-garbed figure suddenly popped out of a doorway across the hall with his submachine gun blasting. Lisa knocked him back into the bedroom with a shotgun blast.

One of the bloodied attackers in the hall was still alive and had an arm left in working condition. He pulled the pin out of a hand grenade with his teeth and threw it at them underhand.

Tommy reversed the grip on his rifle as he leaped into a half-crouch. He swung out at the grenade with the wooden stock of his gun and batted it directly back at the man who had thrown it.

The grenade went off in the wounded hurler's face as Tommy and Lisa ducked the shrapnel behind the wall.

They stood up and moved warily down the hall, walking back-to-back with Lisa covering the rear. Tommy halted when he came to the railed balustrade at the head of the staircase down. He peered around the edge of the wall at the fighting going on below.

There were about six of the Thunder and Lightning firemen left in action. Seven or eight others were lying cut down in the wide entry hall. Bullets were flying out of the rooms and corridors in all directions.

The Mafia guards had fallen back to the cover of the hallways leading off from the entry hall. Once they realized the attackers were wearing armor under the firemen coats, they concentrated their superior firepower on the faces and legs of the invaders and had turned the tide of battle.

The Thunder and Lightning remnants still on their feet were gathered into a clump and backing their way toward the foot of the stairs. They were clearly expecting the rooftop party to come pouring down from above and once more reverse the course of the fight.

One of the firemen looked up, nervously seeking those reinforcements who should have been here already. Tommy had a clear aim and shot him through the forehead.

He and Lisa dropped down to the floor and poured fire across the curving sweep of stairway into the surviving attackers. He had plenty of ammunition, having grabbed a handful of loaded clips out of the belts of the slain gang members in the hall behind him.

Tommy kept up a steady and withering fire as Lisa blasted off with her shotgun, reloaded more shells, and fired again. Caught in a crossfire from above, the final phase of the trap was closed and the T&L men went down in a bloody welter.

The sudden eerie silence as the gun battle ended was strange indeed. Tommy and Lisa hurried down the stairs. Bartlett Delmonico dashed out of a corridor, brandishing .45 caliber revolvers in both hands. Other Mafia leaders poured out behind him, their eyes wild with blood-lust excitement that they carried under the thinnest veneer of social politeness during ordinary circumstances.

Delmonico called out, "Thank God, you're all right, Lisa." He waved his arms toward a side corridor. "This way, everybody. We've got to pull out before cops are all over this place. We're going to our back-up safety house. Ricco, guards, form a phalanx."

Tommy rushed into the knot of mob leaders with Lisa. He had no desire to face any of the Thunder and Lightning snipers most probably stationed out front to mop up. He muttered into Lisa's ear as they ran toward the rear of the mansion, "Back-up safety house, huh? Another one of your surprises?"

"That's right," said Lisa. "There was no need for you to know about it except in case of emergency. That's the whole point of a safe house. And believe me, it's no mansion." She was pumping more shells into her shotgun as she jogged along with her soft breasts bouncing.

The group halted at the left rear corner of the mansion as one of the chief guards scouted ahead. When he signaled with a low whistle, the group burst through a kitchen service exit, crossed a paved backyard and reassembled jumpily in a narrow alley where a barred gate led to an adjoining street.

While the mobsters watched warily overhead for the first sign of a sniper's weapon to come poking over the adjacent roofs and cut them down like sitting ducks, two bodyguards raced out into the street and started up a battered, nondescript Dodge van parked halfway down the block.

The van pulled up in front of the alleyway, the doors to the rear were thrown open, and the Mafia party piled in. The van was moving even before the doors slammed shut again.

Inside the van it was as crowded as a cattle truck, with hips, elbows and gunbarrels poking uncomfortably everywhere. But Tommy noted with approval the slabs of steel armor plating wedged along the sides and roof inside the van compartment.

And the cramped ride was mercifully short, no more than five or six roundabout blocks down toward the base of Pacific Heights' steep hills. Then the van bounced onto a curbside driveway, halted while one of the armed guards in the front seat leaped out and opened a garage door, and then ground to a final stop inside a small household garage.

The garage door went right down again and was bolted from the inside. The gangster bosses and their guards climbed gratefully out of the van. A door at the side of the garage led to an inner stairway.

They ascended into a typical San Francisco townhouse, with about six rooms lined up on either side of a single corridor.

They assembled in the living room behind drawn blinds. The room was at the front of the house and filled the structure's entire width beyond the end of the access corridor. About the only furniture were couches and bare mattresses. But there were plenty of those.

Bartlett Delmonico took his place at the head of the room. "Welcome, gentlemen. You may not have much privacy while we're here but there's plenty of basic comforts. The kitchen is stocked with plenty of food and booze. There's lots of arms and ammo in the closets as well as changes of clothes in most sizes. There's also a fire escape out back in case we need another fast exit."

"I'm not knocking your wisdom in having this refuge set up for us," said a grizzled old Mafiosa. "But now my main concern is getting out of here and returning home."

"Naturally," said Delmonico with his usual smoothness. "Our opponents have effectively halted the need for us to vote on continuing our conference. We shall have to adjourn until the Thunder and Lightning has been completely wiped out by our esteemed friend, Mr. Lee. So we'll only be here long enough to make safe arrangements to fly out. Is that agreed?"

There were unanimous shouts of agreement.

Another mob capo cheerfully sucked at his cigar and said, "You know, these Thunder and Lightning chinks had a couple of good gimmicks with that fire engine bit and the body armor. But if that's the biggest attack they can mount, we ain't got much to worry about. We'll just blow them away every time."

Tommy suddenly spoke up. "The crazy thing is that they could have put a lot more people and heavier weapons into an attack if they wanted to," he said. "Our tong information so far shows that they've got at least five-hundred members, with over half in California. It bothers me that they didn't bring in more force if this really was their all-out onslaught."

"What are you driving at?" queried Delmonico.

"Let me use the phone a second and I'll give you a more complete answer."

Tommy had made a point of remembering the firehouse precinct number marked on the side of the fire engine that attacked the mansion. He dialed information first and got the phone number of the proper firehouse. When he rang the firehouse next, the phone was picked up immediately.

A deliberately noncommittal voice answered, "Hello."

"Isn't this Firehouse 86," said Tommy.

"Yes, what can we do for you?" said the other party.

"Well, if you're a cop who's investigating why anybody would rip off a fire station, I might just be able to tell you where to find a missing fire engine."

The phone voice shot back, "Just one engine or both of them?"

"Both?" said Tommy. "You mean there's two stolen fire engines?"

He slammed down the receiver, having found out all he needed to know there. Immediately he was dialing another number. This time there was no answer, although there should have been people present at any hour of the day or night.

Tommy's face was ashen pale as he hung up the phone again. "That was central tong headquarters I just tried to call," he said. "And it was *two* fire engines Thunder and Lightning stole from the firehouse. I'm afraid I know why there weren't more raiders when they took on your mansion. . . ."

CHAPTER THIRTEEN

"I've got to go," said Tommy grimly. He had to return to Chinatown and tong headquarters at once. Up to right now he would have imagined it unthinkable that Chinese would attack their elders and respected community leaders head-on. But Thunder and Lightning seemed to specialize in the unthinkable and the unspeakable.

He stood up and made his way through the massed forms of the Mafia survivors sprawled out on the mattresses. "Leave word with the East-West Investigations answering service for anything you need from me. I'll check in every few hours," he announced.

Delmonico reached into a drawer beneath a table and tossed Tommy a set of keys. "These go with a Volkswagen parked by the corner."

Tommy caught the keys and said, "Thanks." He raced down the stairs to the street.

The parked Volkswagen was a dented old beetle but Tommy was grateful enough for having some wheels that would keep him from having to waste precious minutes looking for a taxi or stealing another car.

He powered the VW bug across the town's narrow hilly streets to Chinatown as fast as it would go, cutting lights, corners, and lanes with reckless abandon. At one point he ran up on the sidewalk to get around a line of autos waiting for the red light to change.

He left the VW just around the corner from the central tong building and walked rapidly to his destination. Tong headquarters in the center of a crowded block was like some scene out of an old war movie.

There were searchlights of all kinds flashing, lights atop

the police cars, ambulances and fire engines totally clogging the street. A stolen fire engine from the same station as the one that attacked the Pacific Heights mansion was backed up over the sidewalk right up against the tong building and its extension ladder ran alongside the building front even higher than the roof.

The stolen fire engine had clearly been abandoned after the Thunder and Lightning force was through with it. And now it was being used by real firemen along with the rest of their equipment, to fight the smoky flames that were puffing out of the windows on every floor.

Tommy's spirits sank even lower as he saw familiar faces from the tong council being loaded on stretchers into the waiting ambulances. Fierce destruction had obviously been wreaked on this citadel of peaceful community leadership. If only he had been here to help defend it.

As Tommy got closer to the tong building, he saw a flustered San Francisco police captain trying to make some sense out of what had just happened. The captain's investigation wasn't getting anywhere because he was surrounded by tong council members who were shrugging their shoulders, throwing their arms in the air, and jabbering away in Chinese dialects as if they couldn't communicate in English.

This tableau raised Tommy's hopes slightly. If there were surviving council members with enough presence of mind to conceal the tongs' war against the Thunder and Lightning from the cops, perhaps the damage wasn't as bad as it looked.

Tommy walked boldly up to the police captain and flashed his official investigator's badge. "Can you use some help translating, Cap," he asked. "I was just driving by when I saw this mess. What happened?"

"Damned if I know, pal," replied the captain. "I've never seen anything so confused. I'd sure appreciate it if you could get a statement from these guys for me. A departmental translator is on the way but it might be another twenty minutes before he gets here."

"Sure," said Tommy. "Glad to do it."

But before he could turn his attention to a conversation with the tong councilmen, who had been studiously pretending not to recognize him, the captain asked, "This is some kind of Chinatown community building here, isn't it?"

"That's right," replied Tommy. "This is the center for the tong associations of Chinatown."

"Tongs?" said the captain, his eyes starting to widen.

Tommy quickly countered, "These are peaceful community organizations. There hasn't been a tong war in San Francisco for fifty years."

He turned to the councilmen, speaking in rapid Chinese. "Your quick thinking has been most valuable to our cause, respected fathers. This is no matter for police interference. First, you must tell me where is the honorable Lo Sing."

The tiny, wizened Chinaman with the fuzzy white chin-beard who had spoken so eloquently at the first grand council meeting spoke up. "Alas, although I believe Lo Sing is still alive I fear he was kidnapped by the devils of the Thunder and Lightning."

"Oh no," said Tommy, his mouth dropping open.

The old Chinese continued, "The stolen fire engine rammed into the tong house and sent up the ladder. Attackers climbed in through windows on every floor while more of them in other cars were shooting down the guards at the entrance. They threw bottles of gasoline with burning wicks everywhere to cause confusion. The main body of attackers went directly to our council room. We tried to resist and many were shot, I am not sure how many councilmen died. They took Lo Sing, saying he would not be released unless the tongs pledge to give up all attempts to track down the Thunder and Lightning. They burned all the files of information we had prepared so painstakingly and then retreated."

The captain broke in impatiently, "Hey, what's the old guy telling you? Let's have it."

Tommy told him, "Just hold on a second, he's almost done." Switching back to rapid-fire Chinese, he said to the councilmen, "It's a tragedy about the destruction of our information files as well as the despicable kidnapping of Lo Sing. But think now, were there any new pieces of information coming in during the last few hours that might be useful?"

"Yes, Tommy Lee, and perhaps it might be an important clue," said a heavyset council member wearing a conservative suit and tie. "Several hours ago we established conclusively that Bobby Hu's girlfriend is now using the name Rose Harlow and working as a cocktail waitress at the Whacko Dragon lounge in North Beach. And Bobby Hu still comes to see her whenever he can."

"That's something hopeful, at least," said Tommy. "If I can find Bobby Hu through this girl, he would be likely to know where they are holding Lo Sing. . . . But now, listen to me as I tell this police officer a story he can believe about what happened here. In all further questioning when the city translator comes, we must each stick to the same tale."

The councilmen chattered their agreement in a melange of various Chinese dialects.

Tommy turned to the police captain and said, "It was a robbery. One of those crazy youth gangs that have been causing so much trouble in Chinatown lately. They must have stolen a fire engine somehow."

"What did they get away with?" the officer wanted to know.

Here Tommy expanded on actual facts. "The tongs have pension plans for their members, just like American fraternal organizations such as the Elks or the V.F.W. To save some of the older members who don't speak English from having to cash checks at the bank, the tongs offer the option of collecting the weekly old-age benefits here in cash. There's about $25-$30,000 on hand each week. It's kept in a good safe and there's always a guard on duty at the main door. What these nuts did in the fire engine was to bypass the guard by climbing in upstairs from the ladder. They forced some of the people to open up the safe for them and threw around some molotov cocktails just out of general craziness."

"That's too much," said the policeman. "Can any of

these gentlemen describe any of the robbers? Maybe come down to headquarters and look at the photo file?"

"Sorry, but that's impossible," said Tommy regretfully. "The crooks who didn't have their faces hidden under the fire helmets were wearing stocking masks."

The captain thanked him and said he'd wait to see what else the translator could discover. He had Tommy tell the councilmen to stay around and then walked off to confer with some of the other officers.

Tommy had a hurried conversation in Chinese with the councilmen, asking them to take charge of the clean-up without him and to try reconstructing from memory as much as possible of the information files.

Then he moved unobtrusively off the block and hurried around the corner to his borrowed Volkswagen. The Whacko Dragon lounge would still be open for a few hours more.

Not that he expected Bobby Hu or any other Thunder and Lightning member to be out bar-hopping the same night the gang had pulled off two bloody assaults. He had to assume that Bobby Hu was still alive. He hadn't recognized Bobby among the dead at the Mafia mansion attack and apparently none of the gang had been killed during the surprise onslaught on the tong building.

But Tommy wanted to establish himself as soon as possible as an ordinary customer of the Whacko Dragon. And this ordinary customer could not be recognizable as the Tommy Lee famed in Chinatown.

He headed the Volkswagen toward the high-rise that housed East-West Investigations. The VW was a good car for him to be driving tonight, anybody watching the building wouldn't expect Tommy to be in something so different from the flashy wheels he usually piloted.

Still, he drove into the underground garage via a less-used side ramp and looked carefully around for stake-outs as he crossed the parking area to wait for the elevator.

Tommy let himself into his emptied-out office suite and unlocked a room adjoining his personal office. This chamber was the local storeroom for his entire range of special equipment.

There were guns and ammunition of a startling range, ultra-sophisticated electronic snooping devices, cameras and tape recorders, radio systems, and all sorts of identity documents. There was also the makeup kit and extensive wardrobe Tommy used for his mystifying disguises.

Tommy actually used a minimum of makeup to achieve his transformations, relying rather on the attitudes conveyed by his acting skills. Tonight what he did was comb his mod hairstyle straight back on the sides and part it on the top, slicking down the arrangement with a liberal dose of vaseline. A pair of thin rubber circular washers was inserted in his nostrils to broaden the nose and make him look purer Chinese than Eurasian. He finished off by rubbing a layer of instant-suntan dye over his face and hands to darken his distinctive translucent skin quality.

From the full clothing racks around the room he carefully selected a garish punk outfit. The costume started with pointy-toed shoes and seersucker pants, topped with an open-collared mustard yellow shirt and a vinyl imitation-leather jacket. A ridiculously wide-brimmed Superfly hat completed the ensemble.

Tommy looked at himself in the mirror and muttered, "Cool, daddy. You're a real bad dude."

He put the Volkswagen into a parking lot a few blocks from the Whacko Dragon and strutted down the crowded streets of the North Beach entertainment triangle. The Whacko Dragon was one of many undistinguished lounge bars in the pocket where North Beach borders Chinatown.

A pulsating electric sign with a dopey-looking drunken dragon breathing fire announced the club. Inside was the predictable pseudo-Chinese decor trying to disguise the fact that this was simply a fancied-up neighborhood bar.

The place was about half-full, not bad for almost midnight on a mid-week night. But San Franciscans liked to get out and party nights, they had a tradition to keep up. There was a rock band playing the current top forty hits, a bunch of Samoan teenagers from the Mission district. They weren't very good, but fortunately they weren't terribly loud.

A chubby redhead with extremely large boobs came over to take his order. There were four waitresses in the place, all costumed in souvenier-shop silk shirts over hot pants and boots.

"Are you Rose?" Tommy asked her. "Rose Harlow?"

"Nah, that's Rose over there." The redhead gestured toward a much trimmer and more attractive girl getting an order at the bar. "You want her?"

"Sure, we've got mutual friends," said Tommy.

"No sweat," said the redhead. "I'll call her over."

This place was apparently run loosely enough not to be that rigid about things like assigned waitress stations. The redhead went to the bar and told Rose Harlow a customer had asked for her. Then red hopped up on a stool and got into a conversation with the bartender while Rose ambled over.

Rose Harlow was a cute pug-faced dyed blonde whose well-proportioned curves were amply revealed by her brief waitress costume. She was chewing gum and was slightly buck-toothed, but it looked okay on her. She resembled a young and sluttish Doris Day, a fun kid without any mean streaks.

Standing by his table she said, "Hiya, I don't know you. Do I?"

"No, we never met, honey. My pal Joey Tsaing told me to look you up at the Whacko Dragon if I ever got west to San Fran. I'm Terry Lao from New York City."

"Hi Terry." Her brow furrowed as she added, "I don't think I know any Joey Tsaing either."

"That don't surprise me. Joey is a friend of some cat named Bobby Hu and I guess Bobby told him about you. Didn't the two of you go together or something?"

"Oh sure. Bobby and me still go together . . . when he's in town."

"Terrific," said Tommy. "I'm only passing through for a few days myself. Got some business up in Vancouver. But I really like it around here. I might just come back and stay a while."

For the next two hours until closing, Tommy displayed his faked image as a smooth but not overly bright street punk from the East Coast. He didn't come on too strong with Rose or any of the other waitresses, just kidded around and tipped generously for his drinks.

As two A.M. approached, the redheaded waitress asked if he and Rose wanted to join some of the band for coffee at a diner. Tommy acted undecided and when Rose turned down the offer Tommy declined also. Rose said she was too tired for any socializing and would just walk home to her nearby hotel room.

Tommy said goodnight to the girls and informed them he'd probably drop in for a while the next night. Then he went out and waited in a dark doorway to follow Rose. He watched for ten minutes but none of the Whacko Dragon staff came out. He cursed himself for making a stupid lapse and realized that there must be a rear exit everybody left by.

He rushed through the now-quieted streets of North Beach to the rundown little transient hotel Rose had named as where she was staying. He got to the hotel block just in time to see the girl entering the place alone.

Tommy crushed his Superfly hat and shoved it in a pocket. He closed his phony-leather jacket over the garish yellow shirt, removed the widening plugs from his nostrils and shook his hair into an approximation of the usual rumpled style he wore. Then he went into the hotel, engaged the seedy desk clerk in a conversation and slipped him $20 to confirm that nobody was waiting in Rose's room for her. Describing Bobby Hu and leaving word it would be worth $50 to anybody who reported seeing Hu to EWI, Tommy went and picked up his car. He drove around the block behind the Whacko Dragon and checked out the alleyway that led to the rear of the bar. He'd be waiting there after closing tomorrow, with another of his operatives watching the front just in case.

There was nothing else left to do but drive the VW home and get whatever troubled sleep he could despite his worries about Lo Sing in Thunder and Lightning captivity.

He awoke in mid-morning and hurried to the phone to

speak to tong headquarters and check for messages with the East-West Investigations switchboard.

The tong councilman chosen as temporary president had the chilling news that a taped message from Lo Sing had been played over the phone. The kidnapped leader stated that his captors would murder him at the first sign that the tongs were returning to action against the Thunder and Lightning gang. He would be held as hostage for months, if necessary.

Tommy agreed at once that it was too risky to collect any more information about the gang as long as Lo Sing remained in their custody.

He asked only that a re-assembly of the material already collected be delivered secretly to an EWI agent. This was okayed by the council president.

Cousin Lotus told him that Lisa had phoned and left a number at EWI. When Tommy returned the call he found himself connected to the town-house hiding place of the Mafia bosses.

Lisa got on the line and said, "We're starting to move our people out of town in small groups. We decided it would be too obvious to use armored cars, after all. So we've just been sending them out by all kinds of different routes. Bartlett and I will be leaving with the last group and we want to meet with you before we go."

"All right," said Tommy. "I'm working on our best lead yet. I'll be in touch." He swiftly ran down what had happened at tong headquarters and his hopes to trace Bobby Hu within the next few days.

He spent the rest of the day restlessly directing his EWI staff as they took over the investigations of names and addresses supplied by the tongs. He paced the office worrying about Lo Sing and repeating to his operatives how important it was that their efforts remain secret from the Thunder and Lightning.

A little before eleven that night, Tommy was back in his Terry Lao punk guise and sauntering into the Whacko Dragon.

He was greeted as a welcome old friend by Rose and the rest of the waitresses. The night became a replay of his previous visits here. He tipped generously, made bad jokes, and heard more than enough of bad rock music.

The waitresses started dropping word about an after-hours party with some musicians from a Broadway jazz club playing a jam session. Tommy was given an address to go to and said the party sounded good to him. But Rose told the other waitresses she couldn't go because she had a date, and she wouldn't go into any more detail than that although Tommy kidded her about it, carefully avoiding bringing up Bobby Hu's name in his rap.

He left the Whacko Dragon about fifteen minutes before closing, starting to feel increasingly hopeful that Bobby Hu would be showing up. Tommy told the waitresses he'd see them shortly at the jam session.

He stood in front of the Whacko Dragon for a moment so his operative sitting quietly in a car down the block could spot him and make contact if there was anything developing. When nothing happened he went next door to an unlocked office building he'd checked out the previous night.

The Whacko Dragon was a one-story storefront location. Tommy walked upstairs to the second floor of the office building and went to a large hall window that commanded a view of the entire alley behind the nightclub. He pressed himself close to the wall and waited, looking down.

Within five minutes after the 2 A.M. California bar closing hour, the three other waitresses, the musicians, and the bartenders had all passed briskly through the alley and gone down the street. Rose Harlow came out by herself about a minute after the last of the others. Tommy could spot her blonde hair at once.

She walked through the alley a lot slower than the rest had, almost dawdling. Then she looked up at the alleyway wall farther down from where Tommy was hiding.

There was a light clanking of metal and then a shadowy figure was climbing down a fire escape, hanging from the ladder, and dropping down to the pavement.

The figure and Rose Harlow rushed toward each other

and blended into an intense kiss and embrace. Tommy caught a very brief glimpse of the figure's face as it passed through a patch of moonlight on the way to Rose.

Jackpot! It was Bobby Hu.

CHAPTER FOURTEEN

Tommy approved heartily of the passion with which lovebirds Rose and Bobby were kissing and clutching. He hoped Bobby Hu would have his eyes shut during the next minute or so of making out. Because if Bobby wasn't distracted, he would have a very easy shot at a temporarily vulnerable Tommy Lee.

But there was no other way to get at Hu.

Tommy smoothly stepped through the open second-story window and lowered himself silently to arm's length. He was dangling in midair, holding onto the window frame with both hands.

If Bobby Hu had looked up from his heavy-duty kissing, Tommy would have been in clear view. But Tommy wasn't spotted, thanks to the power of love. He let go with his left hand, to let his body lower a few more inches. Then he pushed out from the wall with his near foot.

It couldn't be delayed any longer. Tommy swung himself out so that he would land clearly in the middle of the alleyway and let go. His shoes were about nine feet above the pavement when he started dropping. It was not a jumping height that presented any particular difficulty to Tommy Lee.

On the other hand, it was not a height from which even a Tommy could land in complete silence.

Bobby Hu jerked his head up as he heard the soft thud of Tommy's springing impact. He looked down the alley and saw a crouched human shape dressed like a cheap punk. But he wasn't about to indulge in any detailed examinations before pulling out his gun.

"Hold it, you," said Bobby as he drew. "What the hell is going on?" And then he recognized the familiar face beneath the greased-back hair, the artificial skin tan, and the broadened nose. "My God," he coughed in a panic, "it's Tommy Lee."

Tommy spread his arms outward and called softly, "Bobby, it's okay. We can make a deal. I'm not out to hurt you. Your family were too good friends to me as a kid for that. Just hear me out and I could do you and Rose here the biggest favor you ever had."

"Fuck that," yelled Bobby. "We ain't got nothing to talk about, you half-honkie pig." He snapped out his arm and fired off a hurried shot in Tommy's direction.

But Tommy had already dived forward and was hurling himself low across the twenty feet of space that separated him from Hu. He half-leaped, half-charged in a blur of motion that would have been near impossible to hit except by a calm and expert marksman, of which Bobby was neither.

This time, Tommy's planning made him determined to use his own pistol only in the final extremities of self-defense. A dead or wounded Bobby with a bullet in him would be in no shape to tell Tommy what he so desperately needed to know. And so Tommy did not simply get the drop on Bobby from his vantage point by the window above, which would have been easy enough to do.

As so often before, Tommy would have to rely on his remarkable martial arts capabilities.

Rose Harlow was still standing close to and alongside Bobby, frozen in confusion at this sudden welter of events. Tommy couldn't avoid smashing into her as he ended his spectacular dive for Bobby. She went flying sideways against the nearby wall, slumping down into a sitting position with the breath knocked out of her.

Tommy tackled Hu around the ankles and sent him bouncing down, flat on his back. Another wild shot went off into the air as he fell. Tommy lifted himself up with his arms and catapulted on top of Bobby. He grabbed the tough's gun arm and pushed it back so hard that Bobby's revolver flew out of the grip and bounced ten feet.

At the same time, Tommy snapped the flexed knife-edge of his left palm into the side of Bobby's neck, putting him out cold for the next few minutes. There was no time for more discussion here. He had to get them away before the two gunshots brought uninvited company.

He jumped to his feet and hauled Rose Harlow erect. The bar girl looked at him in wide-eyed fright and whimpered, "I don't get it, Terry. What's going on?"

Intently, but not harshly, Tommy said, "I'll explain to you and Bobby as soon as we get out of here. I'm trying to help the two of you be together all the time instead of having to sneak meetings like this. If I wanted to hurt you I could have shot you down from where I was hiding. Come on."

He picked up Bobby's inert form and slung him over his shoulder. Rose was a little wobbly in the knees so Tommy supported her with his arm around her.

The procession stopped for a moment while Tommy picked up Bobby's pistol, and then continued out into the fortunately deserted street. A powerful Thunderbird auto had been left by Tommy's operatives parked unlocked a few car-lengths from the mouth of the alley.

Tommy dumped Bobby Hu in the back seat with Rose there to comfort him and took off behind the wheel immediately. He drove out of the immediate neighborhood swiftly and circuitously, winding up in the not-quite-empty parking area of that round-the-clock tourist attraction, Fisherman's Wharf.

It was a short ride and Bobby was already starting to come around, as his muttering and squirming in the back seat surely indicated. Tommy instructed Rose to rub Bobby's neck at the base of the skull and in a few moments Hu's eyes started to blink open.

"Take it easy, we're here to talk about a deal," said Tommy quickly before Hu's returning consciousness could throw him into another violent panic. He reached into a pocket and handed Rose a thick envelope.

"That's $10,000 I want to give you," said Tommy. "Rose can start counting it out for you."

Bobby sneered as he said, "Sure, $10,000 for ratting

on the Thunder and Lightning after all they've done for me. What kind of a rotten fink do you think I am?"

"Thunder and Lightning hasn't done shit for you," snapped Tommy in return. "Wise up. They took you in when nobody else would after you made a bad mistake and double-crossed your old friends. But the only reason they helped you out is because they *need* desperate people with nothing to lose and no place to go. Who else would take on all these suicidal missions that are the trademark of the Thunder and Lightning? Anything you owed them for taking you in, you've paid back long ago."

Bobby looked at Tommy without saying anything, but the sneer was starting to fade from his lips. Tommy went on, "You know perfectly well that if you don't get out of the Thunder and Lightning your life expectancy is zero. Now I'm ready to give you a chance to start a new life with your woman here. Rose is a good girl, you're lucky to have her. And she'll be the first to tell you I'm right."

Rose started sniffling, almost on cue. "Oh Bobby," she said, "if only we could get out of town and start over."

Tommy continued boring in, "You're luckier than the rest of those losers in the gang. You aren't wanted by the cops for a major crime. I'll give you this $10,000 from the tongs and you can keep this car too. Start driving now and you'll be halfway to Salt Lake City by sunup. Nobody will ever find you under new names. If you want to repay your old teen gang for stealing their treasury, you can mail in payments through the tongs or my detective agency. Then you won't have anybody on your case."

Bobby was obviously shaken by Tommy's offer. But he said suspiciously, "What happens if I don't tell you what you want to know? You'll just try to beat it out of me, huh?"

"No, I'll just turn you in to the cops as a suspect in the raid on united tong headquarters," said Tommy. "Your pals in Thunder and Lightning will find a way to kill you in jail. They won't be able to break you out and they certainly won't take a chance on leaving you alive to maybe turn state's evidence."

Bobby's face paled as he realized the full implications

of the death sentence Tommy was placing before him. Rose clung to him desperately, pleading with her man to take the money and go off with her.

Tommy waited patiently until Bobby finally sighed and asked, "Okay, what is it you'd want me to tell you for this ten grand?"

Tommy answered, "Only two things."

"Two?" asked Bobby incredulously.

"The first thing," said Tommy, "is where are they holding Lo Sing?"

Bobby Hu took a deep breath and, apparently not wanting to leave himself time to reconsider his decision, he said, "They're holding Lo Sing in the main war bunker Thunder and Lightning has in San Francisco. It's a cellar under a half-block row of storefront units on Hogan Street at the upper end of Chinatown. There's a back way out through a yard on the next street, or you can get in through the little noodle store which is a front for the gang. There's also a connection through the sewer system for emergencies."

Tommy nodded and clasped Bobby heartily on the shoulder for a moment. At last he had enough information to be able to strike back at this gang of madmen. "All right," he said. "The final thing I need to know is who the leaders of the Thunder and Lightning are."

Bobby licked his lips and said, "It's two guys who work together. The only names I know them by are Thunder for one and Lightning for the guy who's around San Francisco most of the time."

Surprised by this news, Tommy said, "What do they look like?"

"Lightning has a zigzag scar on his right cheekbone," answered Bobby. "I guess that's how he got his name. Otherwise he just looks like any other regular Chinese-American hood. So does Thunder, except I think that one's from Asia even though he speaks good English. Thunder walks with a bad limp, but he's real tough. That's really all I know about those two, honest."

Tommy pondered what he had just learned. He fixed on Bobby with an unwavering stare and said, "You better not be lying to me about any of this, Bobby. If I find out you are, despite my respect for your mother and family I guarantee I'll track you down and bust you apart."

"Forget it," said Hu. "If there's one thing that scares me more than Thunder and Lightning ever finding out I ratted on them, it's the idea of having Tommy Lee coming after me. It looks like you're being straight with me, and I'm being straight with you. I haven't forgotten about how it was when we were kids together. And I was pretty shook up when T&L decided to attack the united tongs and nab the council president. That's about as heavy as you can get."

Tommy wished Bobby and Rose luck and left them the big car. Even at this hour of the night it didn't take him long to find a cab parked at the head of Fisherman's Wharf. He had the taxi take him to the East-West Investigations office rather than his apartment.

He caught a few hours sleep on the convertible sofa in his private office and was right there waiting to give his instructions as the EWI staff started coming in after nine a.m.

An operative who specialized in records searches was swiftly dispatched to the city's building department to look up the plans on file for construction of the Hogan Street stores and the cellar beneath.

Meanwhile, other EWI operatives with hidden cameras and telephoto lenses were surreptitiously making a photographic survey of the immediate neighborhood around Hogan Street's secret bunker.

Tommy had copies of the building code plans filed with the city brought back to the office by his searcher well before noon. He and his top team of aides got to work, poring over the blueprints spread all over Tommy's floor and the dozens of photos taped to the walls.

It took three more hours of intense concentration, comparing the plans of the electric and piping systems and the local sewer maps. But at the end they had a plan that everyone agreed had the best chance to work.

The plan called for Tommy to act as a one-man spearhead force, taking a wild chance in order to break into the cellar bunker and whisk out Lo Sing before they realized what was happening and exterminated their hostage. Yet Tommy couldn't accomplish what he needed to do on his own without a great deal of outside help, both as fighters and as decoy distractions.

He set up a mid-afternoon meeting with the acting leaders of the tong council in a place where they would be least likely to be noticed or spotted. And his EWI operatives made sure the tong councilmen weren't followed.

They all got together in one of the private dining rooms of a neighborhood Japanese restaurant in the Little Nippon district.

And Tommy found a pleasant surprise when he saw some unannounced guests the tong council representatives brought with them. . . .

There were three of them, besides the tong councilmen. Hard-faced young Chinese men, barely older than their teens. They were the leaders of the three biggest and were here. "We came to the council yesterday and offered our help in stamping out the Thunder and Lightning. They're our enemies too. We're tired of our best guys run-

This "workman" went into a small grocery shop that most powerful traditional-style youth gangs in Chinatown.
ing us for things the T&L do, we're tired of everybody thinking Thunder and Lightning is the toughest gang in Chinatown. We also are pretty ticked off that they shot up ning off to join those kooks, we're tired of the cops roust- united tong headquarters, that's a slap in the face to the whole community. Now we hear there's some action coming up against the T&L, and we want in. If you need up to a couple of hundred tough and dependable Chinese fighters, you got us."

Tommy grinned and shook the hoodlum boss's hand. "That's just great, because we're going to need a fairly large amount of good manpower if we're going to get Lo Sing out of this alive. And I was wondering how to recruit enough fighters."

He started unrolling some of the blueprints and diagrams he'd brought along. "Now here's what we're going

to have to do in order to avoid a bloodbath. We'll have to strike from three sides simultaneously...."

Early that evening, a rather tall Chinese whose face body was encased in a grimy pair of mechanic's overalls was partially hidden by a floppy baseball cap and whose ambled up Hogan Street carrying two large toolboxes.

The gangs' main spokesman quickly outlined why they was one of the units in this multiple store-front structure. There were two customers in the grocery and they were familiar faces from the central tong council. The grocer came up and said, "Tommy Lee, this is an honor indeed. I am proud that my humble establishment is able to play some small part in the rescue of venerated Lo Sing."

"Thank you, sir," said Tommy. "I must get right to work. Would you show me where your air duct pipes are in the back of the store?"

"Follow me, please," said the grocer. He led Tommy into his crowded storage room where boxes and cans were piled almost to the ceiling.

Almost exactly where Tommy's municipal blueprints would have led him to look was the narrow, rectangular metal piping of the heating ducts system. As he had hoped, the opening vents that allowed the hot air to escape when the boiler was in use were grilles held in place by nuts and bolts.

"I never had any idea there was a big cellar below here," the old grocer was saying. "Our landlord owns the noodle shop which you say is a front for the Thunder and Lightning gang. The boiler is in a shed behind the building. As a matter of fact, none of the legitimate tenants have been here more than a year. Because that's when this structure was renovated after getting so old and delapidated it was almost condemned and torn down."

"Well, our plans show that there's still a connection where these pipes go into the pipe system from an old boiler down below," said Tommy. "And even if that connection has been sealed up, I've got the tools to break through."

As he spoke, he was unscrewing the vent grille with a

screwdriver. He removed the grille and laid it down on the floor. He opened up his pair of toolboxes and removed the bulging canvas bags that completely filled each one. With a stout cord he tied the bags together, one behind the other. He would be dragging this vital cargo with him through the pipe system.

Tommy shoved the bags in through the grille in the direction opposite to where he'd be going. He piled up three grocery boxes below the grille, stepped up, and laboriously squeezed himself into the pipe tubing.

He waved goodbye to the grocer and the tong councilmen and crawled ahead. He knew he had to hurry. The other attack teams would be striking in exactly forty-five minutes. That was the way it had to be.

The vent pipes were an extremely snug fit, but according to the construction diagrams on file with the city the space was just large enough to enable someone of Tommy's size to slither through. He had a miners' flashlight strapped around his forehead to enable him to see where he was going and he moved his body carefully and deliberately in order to keep as silent as possible. This silence would be even more important as he got closer to the basement.

Tommy had arranged a simple way of signaling the councilmen waiting back in the grocery storage room. He had a ball of narrow string that he unwound as he moved along. A dab of wax marked every ten feet along the string, which would also enable him to know how far along he was. Four pulls on the string would reveal when he had reached his ultimate position, and three pulls would signal if he was in trouble.

Fortunately, the evening was warm enough so that there wasn't any hot air being forced through these pipes. That would have made a fatiguing job even more difficult.

The first section of pipe that Tommy had to traverse crossed the back of three other stores. Tommy shoved himself through the tight tubes at a steady pace, trying to be as quiet as possible. He could only count on the occasional muffled scraping sounds he couldn't help making to be shrugged off as normal plumbing rattles by anyone who happened to be within earshot.

After he counted off 120 feet of string markers he started to feel around for the branch in the vent system that led down into the cellar. He gave a quiet sigh of relief as the angled pipeline turned up right where the blueprints said it should be and then set about unscrewing the filter grille and shoving it aside.

The pipe channel raked downward at a steep angle. Tommy had to brace his elbows and feet hard against the side in order to keep from sliding down in a headlong clatter. Sweating and gritting his teeth, he proceeded carefully down the slide. It had required all of his remarkable body control and endurance to get this far.

At the bottom of this drop, the angle gentled out somewhat. Tommy proceeded with special care as he approached the pipes' approach into the cellar. His headlight caught the metallic reflection barring his way just before his groping hands would have banged into it.

A sheet of iron was covering the mouth of the pipe. Tommy's preparations had taken this possibility into account. It made sense for those who planned this hidden bunker to separate their heating system from the vents that fed the stores above.

Tommy rolled onto his back and got the nearest sack open. He removed a diamond-pointed drill and silently put a hole into the metal plating. When he was done, he placed his eye carefully to the opening and was reassured to see nothing but more darkness beyond.

This meant that the pipe system continued on the other side of the sheet of metal, rather than emptying directly into the cellar where he could be seen if he proceeded further. He replaced the drill in his sack and exchanged it for a small but powerful blowtorch.

With the torch he swiftly cut a circle in the metal plate big enough for him to crawl through. He laid the metal discard out of his way and squeezed through tensely. He couldn't allow more than the slightest sound the rest of the way.

According to his calculations, he was now into the vent

pipes that ran along the cellar's side walls where it met the ceiling. He inched along with his sacks, peering up ahead for the nearest grille opening. It took him another twenty-five nerve-wrenching feet of crawling before he saw the pattern of light coming in ahead.

He peered through the grille and found he had a view of over half of the sprawling cellar room. The bunker was dimly lit and to his surprise there were only about twenty men in view. He spotted Lo Sing, blindfolded and bound to a chair in the corner. This was particularly important. He'd need to get to Lo Sing fast when the action started.

Tommy checked his watch. He was in position nearly five minutes early. He gave four strong tugs to the string that had marked his passage down here and felt the answering tugs. Silently he turned on his side and began assembling his weapon from the second sack.

Meanwhile, on the crowded tourist thoroughfare that was Hogan Street up above, one of Chinatown's most spectacular visual treats began to make its way closer to the bunker....

It was a traditional Chinese wedding procession, complete with a long, fabric dragon that covered a lot of striding legs as it humped and snaked its way down the gutter. The large wedding party had perhaps a disproportionate amount of slick-looking young men with hard eyes. But there were enough jolly old folks on hand to make the thing look genuine.

And to make the whole thing even more colorful, the procession marchers were dressed in bright and flowing Chinese silk robes. These loose robes served excellently to cover the many guns the youthful marchers were wearing as well as their military bulletproof body armor. It was a good idea Tommy had cheerfully appropriated from the fake-firemen attacks made by the Thunder and Lightning gang a few nights back.

Every wedding naturally needed a bride and groom, of course. So there was a handsome pair being carried along in the traditional sedan chair. The radiant bride was Tommy's own Cousin Lotus and at her side was EWI detective Harry Chow.

They waved cheerfully at the amused bystanders right up until the time when one of the men carrying the sedan chair, who seemed to have drunk a little too much, stumbled. The procession came to a halt right in front of the very noodle shop that housed one of the secret entrances to the cellar bunker.

Laughing and lurching drunkenly, three of the wedding marchers stomped into the noodle shop to offer the two shopkeepers there a drink from their whiskey bottle.

And this whole complicated charade paid off, as the unsuspecting shopkeepers, who might have flashed some electronic warning to the desperadoes in the cellar below, were swiftly grabbed and their mouths covered.

A clump of wedding merrymakers blocked the view through the shop's street window while the leader of the trio that had captured the shopkeepers placed a razor-sharp knife blade against the throat of one of the captives and said, "I'm going to count to five. And if you don't tell me how to open the passage to the cellar, I'll slit both your throats."

Ominously he counted to five and, when neither man nodded his head in signal he was giving in, the knife man drew his blade across the neck of the shopkeeper, leaving a red new mouth line of dripping blood.

CHAPTER FIFTEEN

As the second shopkeeper saw the blood running out of his partner's throat, his eyes rolled in panic. He began pumping his head up and down and trying to speak behind the firm hand that was covering his mouth.

When his mouth was uncovered, he blurted out, "You pull out a rack of goods on the left wall ... the second rack, it covers a door.... Please, don't kill me too. We aren't members of the Thunder and Lightning, we just watch this store for them."

What the informer didn't know was that the youth gang leader with the knife had only broken the surface skin of the other shopkeeper's throat. A Chinese nurse with the wedding party would quickly close up the frightening but minor wound with bandages.

The spearhead trio waved the rest of the attack party into the shop and rushed into the back room. The rack of shelves holding imported Chinese pasta swung forward just as described. Beyond was a short staircase leading down to the cellar.

The attack started with four tear gas bombs being thrown down the staircase in rapid order.

Then the tough youth gang fighters and Tommy's EWI detectives pulled on their gas masks and charged down the steps in their body armor, shooting as soon as they got to the cellar.

As soon as Tommy saw the first puffs of acrid tear gas smoke pouring out of the bombs, he snapped his own gas mask in place and started shooting a cloud of tear gas through the grille.

He had brought along a cannister tank of the chemical

and now released it through a hose and cone arrangement pressed against the grille.

In a matter of seconds, the tear gas surprise attack had filled the entire room with a dense, choking smoke that made vision next to impossible beyond point-blank range. Isolated gunfire was heard in the room, but not that much because nobody could really see well enough to pick out a target.

Most of the noise filling the smoky chamber was groaning and retching as the gas did its work, interspersed with shouted instructions by the desperate defenders.

So far, so good. Tommy had carefully loosened the inside nuts holding the grille in place. Now he dragged himself into position and sent the grille flying open with one powerful kick. He shoved his legs through the opening and dropped to the floor.

With his back to the wall, he estimated the angle that would take him to the corner where Lo Sing was held bound to a chair. He had to work as fast as possible. Inhaling a lot of the choking tear gas could be dangerous for an aging man, even a tough old bird like Lo Sing. Although the gas was not chemically designed to be fatal, breathing in enough in an enclosed space like this cellar could well cause suffocation.

Tommy ran crouched over to aid in making himself a smaller target for any stray bullets. He slammed aside any human shapes he ran into, not able to take time to determine who was friend and who was foe.

Soon his outstretched fingers found the wall that must run at right angles from the wall he had entered through. He reached around but could feel no sign of Lo Sing. Swiftly he began to move along the wall, in the right direction for the corner unless he had gotten completely turned around in the smoke.

In ten paces he heard the sound of high-pitched coughing. His frantically waving hand made contact with a blindfolded face and then a wiry body tied to a chair. Lo Sing.

Tommy pulled an extra gas mask from a pouch inside his overalls and strapped it in place over Lo Sing's face.

By the time he had the mask completely adjusted the tong president's intense coughing had turned encouragingly into deep breathing.

Only then did Tommy lean over and whisper into Lo Sing's ear, "It's Tommy Lee. We're getting you out of here behind a gas attack by the Chinatown youth gangs and my detectives. Just take it easy."

Lo Sing nodded his understanding and made himself relax, awaiting whatever his rescuer did next.

Another of Tommy's coverall pockets had a sturdy sheath-knife and Lee guided himself by touch in cutting through the ropes that held Lo Sing to the chair.

He left on the blindfold. It would do little good to remove it in this smoke-fogged room and the cloth was probably protecting Lo Sing's eyes from severe discomfort.

He pulled Lo Sing erect and halfway held him up with an arm pressed firmly around his waist. Lo Sing managed to shuffle along as Tommy dragged him forward, starting to follow the walls back to the entry stairway.

But the struggling pair only took a couple of steps before an intruder loomed through the fog, blocking their way. It was a wild-eyed ruffian holding a wadded jacket in front of his mouth to keep out some of the gas smoke.

The mysterious intruder barked out in a cloth-muffled voice, "No, they won't bring you out alive, traitor hostage." His fog-shrouded arm gave out with a gunflash. But Tommy had whirled Lo Sing back out of the way and the bullet went wild.

Before the gunman had a chance to line up another shot, Tommy had leaped on him, letting go of Lo Sing for the moment. They grappled in the fog, the gunner resisting Tommy's hold with far more power than the great kung fu fighter was used to meeting in his opponents.

But the gunner had to drop the wadded jacket from his face to hold off Tommy in the struggle. And in the next instant, Tommy knew that he had his hands on the mysterious master criminal known only as Lightning!

Not only that, he knew the secret of Lightning's true identity!

Just as Bobby Hu had described it, there was a jagged, zigzag scar puckering Lightning's otherwise ordinary Chinese face into a memorably grotesque mask. The scar tore across Lightning's cheek from his eyelid to his upper lip.

But Tommy also recognized the face disfigured by this scar. It was the face of a vicious Los Angeles hoodlum specializing in Chinatown extortion rackets, who had then been known as only Chooey.

Tommy had lost track of Chooey years ago and assumed the cruel young racketeer had simply dropped into a quieter life or gotten killed.

Ever since Bobby had described the real Thunder and Lightning leaders as a scarface and a cripple, Tommy had been fruitlessly trying to figure out who they might be. He knew of hundreds of oriental criminals since his career started with U.S. Army Intelligence at the age of nineteen.

He could think of a dozen scarred men and a dozen other men who walked with limps that met Bobby's general description. But none of the men he knew of had the brains and determination to launch something as large-scale and deadly as the Thunder and Lightning gang.

As a matter of fact, that went for Chooey too.

Back when Chooey was active shaking down businessmen in Los Angeles, he had been admittedly a tough and cunning hoodlum. But he wasn't anything extraordinary, nothing at all like this.

He struggled hand-to-hand now with Tommy, holding on with remarkably intense determination. Here was no run-of-the-mill ruffian, but a man operating at the peak of his capabilities and holding fast to some implacable purpose. Something besides his ugly scar had caused this huge change in the Chooey Tommy once knew.

Even if the pair had started out fighting on even terms, it is unlikely that Chooey could have resisted Tommy's vise grip on his arms for very much longer. But as it was, Tommy had on a gas mask to keep the tear gas from getting to him while Chooey-Lightning was choking, sputtering and sobbing as the gas attacked his unprotected head.

It was remarkable that he managed to hold off Tommy Lee even this long, his eyes blazing wildly through their irritated tears. He, of course, had no way of knowing who he was fighting behind the face-covering gas mask. And he was starting to bend over backwards so that Tommy would soon be able to pin him to the floor and slug him unconscious.

It was then that random luck came to Lightning's aid.

One of Tommy's men in a gas mask came charging out of the concealing smoke. He accidentally rammed into Tommy, knocking him momentarily off-balance.

Swift as a striking snake, Lightning squirmed free of Tommy. Letting go of his pistol, he jammed his knee into the groin of the man who had stumbled into them and snatched off his gas mask.

Before Tommy could untangle himself from the body falling into him, Lightning had backed away into the smoke. His mad laughter cut through the muffling of the gas mask for a moment and then he was swallowed up in the dense mist.

Tommy couldn't take a chance on pursuit. He had to make sure Lo Sing got out safely.

Backing off to the wall once more, he found Lo Sing sitting huddled into a ball. He got the tong chief to his feet and started moving him toward the exit again.

There was fighting raging all around them. With the still-thick smoke shield there was no real way to determine who was winning. The only odd thing he was aware of was that the surprised Thunder and Lightning defenders seemed to be doing a remarkably self-disciplined job of fighting on despite the tear gas effects.

And then another unhappily familiar shape was looming up ahead of them. Even the thick smoke couldn't disguise the metallic gleam of Hatchet Wang's gleaming namesake weapon and his grotesque silver nose.

Obviously half-crazed and disoriented by the tear gas, Wang lurched erratically forward, brandishing his hatchet at anything that moved.

This was no time for Tommy to go up against the great hatchet man again. Even if Wang didn't know what he was doing at the moment, his endurance and berserk panic with his razor-sharp weapon made it imperative that Tommy keep Lo Sing well beyond the range of Wang's flashing blade.

As Wang stumbled forward, almost on them, Tommy grabbed for the automatic holstered under his coveralls and blasted off a shot at Wang. Even at this nearly point-blank range, it was almost impossible to judge distance accurately enough for a proper aim in the smoke.

Tommy's bullet went wildly to the side and Wang backed off. The sound of the close miss pulling him together enough to realize he had to get out of the way. Wang scuttled back to be hidden once more by the tear gas smoke.

Just before Wang disappeared from sight, Tommy thought he caught a glimpse of a figure with a gas mask dragging Wang farther away. But he couldn't be sure.

So Tommy plunged further ahead, half-carrying and half-dragging Lo Sing. By now the swirling smoke was at last starting to settle and Tommy could see struggling figures emerging out of the murk.

He also saw that he had almost overshot the stairwell leading up to the noodle shop and he swerved hard to the right in order to reach the bottom landing.

And there a bunch of figures in gas masks and body armor were waiting to slap Tommy on the back in heartfelt congratulations and hustle him with Lo Sing upstairs.

Not too much later, Tommy was back at central tong headquarters in one of the rooms that hadn't been damaged by the recent arson. The office had been converted to a temporary infirmary to treat those wounded in the fray.

Many wounded were, in fact, straggling in with small groups and only gradually was the detailed picture emerging of what had happened in the cellar bunker under smoke cover.

Slightly under half of the thirty or so Thunder and Lightning gang members that Tommy had estimated were in the bunker managed to escape through the trapdoor into the sewers.

Among those who escaped were Lightning himself and Hatchet Wang. Naturally Tommy had stationed an interception party to ambush anyone escaping through the sewer. But in the murky darkness the would-be ambushers had made the mistake of stationing themselves too far down the tunnel from where the secret escape hatch turned out to lead into it.

The determined and desperate escapees managed to hold off the snipers with heavy gunfire and fall back in good order through the sewers.

The other largest percentage of Thunder and Lightning members were shot down as they attempted to escape through the exit that opened onto a neighboring yard. Tommy's force had the yard completely pinned down under fields of crossfire. But unanimously the T&L fanatics preferred to shoot back in the face of certain death rather than throw down their arms and surrender.

Those few gang members who didn't make it out of the gas-filled cellar by either route didn't survive either. From all reports, Lightning had remained in the cellar until the last possible moment seeing to that.

Since Lightning had a stolen gas mask on, nobody realized until it was too late that he was not part of the tong raiders as he spirited down to the sewers those of his men who were still able to walk before the gas clouds dissipated. And before he made his final daring escape he put bullets through the heads of his men who were unable to get away.

But even if the raid produced no live captives, it had still succeeded in freeing Lo Sing at the cost of only one youth gangster's life. Thanks largely to Tommy's provision of lightweight bulletproof vests, most of the wounds to the tong fighters were not serious.

As for Lo Sing himself, one of the sympathetic Chinese doctors recruited by the tongs to handle the improvised infirmary had just given him an injection to put him to sleep.

Previously, Lo Sing's lungs had been pumped clean to get rid of the residue of tear gas. "He's weakened from all he's been through," said the doctor. "Although he's basically in sound shape, this is no young man any more."

"I understand all that, Doctor," Tommy protested. "But it's vitally important that we find out anything he knows as soon as possible."

"Believe me, he's in no shape to give you any coherent answers right this minute," countered the doctor. "Let him rest under sedation for just a couple of hours and then I'll let you wake him up to question him. As a matter of fact, I'll even give him a pep-up shot to bring him around then if necessary. But as of this moment, he's got to have sleep."

Tommy had no choice but to go along with the diagnosis. He wandered restlessly around the infirmary for a while, thanking the happily chattering survivors. And then he thought of calling the East-West Investigations answering service to find out if there were any important messages that came in while he was crawling through the heater vents.

It turned out that a Miss Lisa Delmonico had phoned and left a number.

Tommy dialed the Mafia town house hideout and asked for Lisa. When she got on the line, she said, "Well, Bartlett and I are pulling out. Everybody else at the conference has already flown home safely. Why don't you come over and ride out to the airport with us so we can go over the situation en route?"

This was fine with Tommy. It would give him something to do while Lo Sing was resting and he ought to be back in plenty of time to ask his questions. "I'm on the way," he said and left the battered but bustling tong central headquarters.

CHAPTER SIXTEEN

Tommy had to pass through a gauntlet of fresh new guards parked in front of the town house before he was let inside. He was good-humored about it this time, not really caring all that much if they let him by or not.

He found the previously mattress-crowded upper floor practically deserted. Bartlett Delmonico and Lisa were finishing the packing of their final suitcases.

"I see you've brought in some new players," said Tommy.

"You mean the boys downstairs, they're prime local talent," said Delmonico. "Once the conference was down the tubes there wasn't any sense in keeping up security against the San Francisco organization. The locals did a fine job getting our people out smoothly."

He left the bedroom to make sure the car was done loading. As soon as Tommy and Lisa were alone, she said, "I wish you'd have come earlier. We could have had a little time alone again." She pouted her pretty disappointment at losing out on a high-voltage quickie with Tommy tonight.

"I was only able to pick up your message just before," said Tommy politely. "We've been pretty busy tonight in Chinatown."

"Oh? Have you finally gotten a breakthrough?" She was instantly all business and power drive once again.

"Could be. I'll know better how much we've got in a couple of hours. . . . Why don't I go over it in the car with your husband too, so I don't have to repeat myself."

Bartlett shouted up the stairs that they were ready to go. Waiting in the garage when Tommy and Lisa descended was an extra-long Cadillac limousine with a mob driver-gunner at the wheel.

Bartlett Delmonico got into the back seat, but Lisa climbed in the front next to the driver and beckoned Tommy to sit on the outside by her. Delmonico wound up sitting behind the driver with another mobster who was flying in their chartered jet with them as far as the East Coast and a second bodyguard by the other window.

The garage door was opened and the car parked in the driveway led off. Before they got to the corner they were picked up and followed by a second protective car parked down the block.

The trim little automotive procession made its way downhill from Pacific Heights. Tommy explained in detail what had happened during the raid on the Thunder and Lightning cellar bunker and how he hoped that Lo Sing would soon be able to provide a lot more solid information.

When Tommy was done, Bartlett Delmonico commented, "Well, we certainly can't make any complaints about how much you've managed to accomplish, so far. With half of the Thunder and Lightning top leadership identified and one of their main San Francisco bases cracked, it definitely would seem that you're making good progress. And we'll keep our commitment to build a new Chinatown community center when you succeed."

As he was talking, Lisa quietly leaned up against Tommy in the front seat. With one hand, she clutched his groin and with her other hand she grabbed his wrist and tried to shove Tommy's fingers under her skirt.

Tommy pulled away in annoyance. Quickies were one thing and his series of offbeat interludes with this strange Mafia princess hadn't turned him off any. But fooling around in a full car with the lady's husband in the back seat was too furtive and too close for comfort.

Lisa frowned at the rejection and sat up straight in the center of the seat. Tommy filled the silence by asking Delmonico how to get in touch with him in the East if there was anything special to report.

They were heading down in caravan through a quiet

commercial district of small factories and warehouses to climb onto the handiest freeway entrance.

It was one of San Francisco's typically narrow one-way streets. A large truck had pulled around the corner in front of the procession. Nothing unusual about that. Plenty of trucks operating around this district, even at night.

The lead car picked up a little speed to pass the truck on the right. This was a large, unmarked 7½-ton truck, about as big as you get without going into trailer and rig. It was going just slowly enough so that the lead car driver didn't see any point in letting the procession dawdle behind it to the freeway.

But as the lead car came alongside the truck, the bigger vehicle suddenly angled right and started to pull in front of the auto, forcing it to brake and swerve toward the curb.

The limousine Tommy was riding in and the car bringing up the rear had to jam on the brakes instantly to avoid a total pile-up. Only the expertise of the three local Mafia drivers brought the cars sliding and screeching to a halt with no more damage to each other than a slight nudging of bumpers.

Tommy knew this had to be an ambush of some sort, and a particularly tricky one. Even as the limousine he rode in was rocking to a stop he was peering around in all directions to try to get a fix on where the attack would be coming from.

Besides the truck that had blocked them off, there didn't seem to be anybody else lurking in the shadowy street. Yet Tommy knew that there had to be more than one vehicle, plus probably a two-way citizens band radio contact, in order for the truck to have been ready to pull in front of them en route.

And then the U-Haul orange rent-a-van came screeching up behind them. None of the Mafia shotgun riders had even the time to climb out of their autos before the side panel of the boxy little van slammed open and a bazooka rocket launcher was being pointed in their direction.

At the same instant, the rear doors of the larger truck flew apart and a machine gun unit set in position on its metal legs opened up a chattering rain of death bullets.

The bazooka man apparently did not have a clear line of fire at the limousine amid the welter of vehicles from his post in the van. He hopped out nimbly and lurched to the side with an extremely rapid gait despite an obviously dragging limp of one leg. In the shadowy street, his lopsided gait and unbalanced rocket-gun load made his dim outline look like a prancing demon from hell.

It was this split-second delay of the bazooka blast that saved Tommy's life. He saw what was coming and had barely time enough to duck down under the dashboard, dragging Lisa down with him.

The bazooka shell ripped into the rear end of the limousine, shredding Bartlett Delmonico and the other two passengers into a crimson instant pulp.

But their bodies and the padding of the front seat kept any of the shrapnel from reaching through to Tommy and Lisa. Tommy kicked open the door handle with his foot and slid out to the gutter. "Hurry up, if you're coming," he shouted to Lisa.

He rolled to his feet alongside the car and dashed for cover behind the few trucks left parked overnight on the opposite sidewalk. Out of the corner of his eye he could see another tough-looking little Oriental popping a second shell into the rear of the bazooka.

Tommy was blocked by the front cars from most of the machine gun fire from the trucks. Only a couple of hand guns were shooting vainly at him from the van as he ran.

There was something about the fast but jerky limp with which the bazooka man had moved into position that stirred Tommy's memory sharply. But of course he had no time now to consider it.

Over all the noise of the shooting, he could hear Lisa running along behind him at a rapid clip, hardly even breathing hard as she came. Tommy didn't bother looking back. It was up to Lisa to save her own life, all he would do for her was lead the best way to get under cover.

He felt no further sense of duty to the lovely but power-crazed Mafia princess.

They got behind the multiple tires of a parked truck trailer just as the second bazooka shell ripped into the limousine. This time there was a direct hit on the gas tank and the whole car burst into flames.

It would be only a matter of minutes before the two surrounding cars caught fire too and ultimately exploded.

The ambush truck fired some more bursts of machine gun fire around the area but it had to get out of range of the coming explosion and started to roll forward.

The bazooka man gimped forward in Tommy's direction. He was reloaded again and setting himself in position to fire off a shell close enough to Tommy and Lisa to blow them apart.

But Tommy had no reason to just crouch there and let it happen. He snatched his Colt .45 out of the shoulder holster and blasted out three rapid shots that barely missed the bazooka wielder as he attempted to kneel down into firing position. One of Tommy's bullets actually hit the side of the bazooka tube and clanged off.

Over Tommy's shoulder, he heard Lisa clicking open the oversized purse she carried and removing some bulky object. A few seconds later, a thunderous roar suddenly went off almost in his ear and a small patchwork of blood-red dots appeared in the side of the bazooka man's shirt as he lurched backwards, knocked out of balance.

Lisa was muttering, "Damn, I only caught him with a few pellets at the outer edge of the pattern."

As Tommy snapped his head around, he saw Lisa cradling a menacing sawed-off shotgun with a snap-on wooden stock and taking a better aim at the bazooka man.

"You're full of little surprises, aren't you?" Tommy grumbled as his eardrum throbbed annoyingly from the unexpected sound blast.

But the bazooka man now had enough. He was not about to plant himself and aim his rocket from an unprotected open stance under the fire of a pistol and a shotgun. He scuttled backwards with his game leg dragging and disappeared behind the side of the van as Lisa loosed her second shot.

The van backed up at full speed and u-turned to rush off in the opposite direction from the bigger ambush truck. Three of the local Mafia bodyguards had survived the gun barrage and they came staggering away from the burning cars to rejoin Tommy and Lisa.

Not wasting time on talk, the battered quintet jogged down the block and turned the corner just as the autos started to explode in a series of roaring blasts.

An aging station wagon was parked on the block. One of the bodyguards broke in and swiftly hot-wired it to start. The fivesome all jumped in and rolled out of the neighborhood before it filled up with onlookers, firemen, and cops.

After a minute the driver turned down onto Market Street and he asked Lisa, "Where to now? The airport? Your Lear jet's still waiting."

Lisa's face betrayed no tears of either fear or mourning. She looked grim and implacable, and in some way rather pleased. "No, back to the town house for tonight and then tell Don Ricco in Oakland to expect a house guest in his compound. It was never my vote that we run out of town before this fight was over."

She looked like a bacchante or fury, one of the ancient demi-goddesses of violence and carnage. She turned to Tommy and announced, "I'm staying right here until the Thunder and Lightning is out of business. The command of Bartlett Delmonico's forces is rightfully mine and I intend to hold onto it. You have got until the end of the week to lead me to the headquarters of the Thunder and Lightning gang or I'll put a price on your head of $250,000."

"You can keep your threats," replied Tommy angrily. "You remember the word from the tongs about what would happen if any Chinese were hurt in reprisals."

"I'm not talking about reprisals on Chinese hostages taken off the streets," she said. "I'm talking about you personally and a quarter of a million dollars to any hitman who gets you, if you don't deliver."

The car halted for a red light and Tommy threw his door open and stepped out. "This is far enough. I'll get back to Chinatown on my own," he said coldly. "I'll keep in touch, lady."

Lisa was calling after him, "See that you do." But Tommy was walking rapidly up the hill and didn't stop to listen to her.

When he got back to central tong headquarters he found that Lo Sing had already awakened naturally and was being fed some soup broth while he waited impatiently for Tommy's return.

"I'm glad to see you feeling better," said Tommy.

"I owe thanks to you for that," Lo Sing replied. "I know they would have eventually killed me if you hadn't brought about a rescue."

"I am grateful for your kind words. Have the police been here yet? I saw many patrol cars in Chinatown tonight."

"Yes, they came into the building and asked many questions. But they did not search every room and thus this infirmary clinic remained hidden. It was certainly to be expected that the police would look into the possibility that tonight's big gunfight was somehow connected with the earlier attack on this building. But our tong councilmen used well their purported ignorance of the English language to pass the police translator as little information as possible."

"Most excellent," said Tommy. "And now, what information did you overhear during your captivity which will help us strike again at the berserk men of the Thunder and Lightning?"

"Of course. I have learned of things that will almost certainly be of great use," began Lo Sing. "But in many other areas my knowledge is very limited. You must understand that I was kept blindfolded almost all the time and so am unable to describe the faces of many of my captors."

"But did they cover your ears, wise Lo Sing?" said Tommy.

Lo Sing grinned broadly, "No, indeed they did not

cover my ears. This is because all but the most elementary of their conversation was carried out in other Asiatic languages besides Chinese. They spoke in Thai and Korean, but mostly in Vietnamese. However, they could have no way of knowing that many years ago, before entering the United States, I lived in Saigon under the French. I found that I soon remembered how to understand the language again."

"Vietnamese, hmm?" This was most welcome news to Tommy because it now helped confirm what he had first begun to suspect when he saw the limping bazooka expert earlier that night. There was a known Vietnamese criminal with a napalm-maimed leg and a skill with portable howitzers who might be a top suspect for the identity of Thunder now. Tommy would be surer when he had a chance to check his widespread office files against the memories of his long-ago Army Intelligence days.

Lo Sing was continuing now. "What they talked about in Vietnamese was their final preparations to bring into San Francisco a huge load of pure heroin, perhaps the biggest drug shipment ever brought into the United States according to their descriptions."

"That is something indeed," said Tommy. "How is this huge heroin shipment coming in?"

"It is in the bottom of a Japanese-registered ship, the *Sakamura*," said Lo Sing. "A false bottom has been constructed in the hull, a large hidden chamber between the bilge of the cargo hold and the outer surface of the ship."

"And how do they remove the heroin within the harbor?" was Tommy's next question.

"It is done entirely underwater, by scuba divers at night," Lo Sing said. "The secret chamber is not accessible from inside the boat. But under the hull, several metal plates screw off easily. These plates are removed by the divers and the heroin packages already in waterproof containers are taken out, tied to floats to neutralize their weight underwater and towed away to a motorboat at a pickup point. The hull plates are then simply screwed back into place. It doesn't matter that the secret compartment fills with water and just adds a bit more weight to the bilge ballast."

Tommy pondered this fascinatingly simple yet effective method of smuggling large cargoes of contraband. With sufficient resources, access to a ship and trained scuba divers, it seemed a practically foolproof technique.

"This is the Thunder and Lightning's most important heroin shipment so far," Lo Sing continued. "It has taken them many months of delays to set up a more roundabout smuggling network out of Bangkok, since the fall of Vietnam has made it impractical to ship Vietnamese heroin direct from a Saigon that is now Communist."

"You have done brilliantly well, Lo Sing," said Tommy happily. "The only detail that remains is to learn the exact arrival time of the ship, *Sakamura*. And that can be easily determined from the record logs of the port authorities."

"Oh, but that will not be necessary," Lo Sing said. "I overheard the entire schedule. The *Sakamura* is steaming just outside the bay now and will be docking early in the morning. The legitimate cargo will begin unloading tomorrow and the divers come to remove the heroin at midnight." The tong chief beamed. "Have I not accomplished my task properly?" he asked.

"More than properly," said Tommy. "So we've got until midnight tomorrow? That should be enough time for preparations."

He excused himself from Lo Sing and grabbed the nearest phone. He dialed through to Lisa Delmonico at her town house bastion and said, "Get as many of your local tough-boys as you can together for tomorrow night. We'll have some shooting to do."

CHAPTER SEVENTEEN

It was pitch-black, bone-chilling cold and wet in the murky waters swirling under the piers of the fabled Port of San Francisco. The tide was a living, pulsating force awaiting even the slightest opening to draw an unwary diver down into the muck-slimed bottom.

Tommy Lee had been stationed here in silence for over two hours.

A sleek, black rubber wet-suit over thick thermal underwear kept the cold from being more than mildly uncomfortable. It had soon become too wearing to continue resisting the tide by holding onto a mossy dock piling, minute after minute. So Tommy had long ago solved the problem by tying a loop of rope around his waist and knotting the other end around the piling to anchor himself.

The darkness of the waters under the shadowed docks made a perfect camouflage for Tommy on this moonless night. He had his head up above the waterline. Nobody could see him unless they came by right above him. And it was pointless to waste the compressed air in the scuba tanks on his back before he needed to go into action.

It had been necessary for Tommy to get into the water and in position several hours before midnight because of all the special equipment he had brought with him. The Thunder and Lightning diving team would have a couple of nasty surprises in store when they came to get the heroin.

He had approached the dock underwater a little before ten p.m. He found the dangling wire alongside the prearranged piling and hooked up his cable transmitter. He also had a regular wireless miniature radio on his belt as back-up. But the earlier signals would be relayed by cable to avoid overhearing by any Thunder and Lightning electronic monitors.

As soon as he set the wires into his first transmitter, he checked it out by tapping a random rhythm on the sending key. At once he got back an answer of random pulsations that sounded a low buzzing which couldn't be heard six feet away from the transmitter. As a former military intelligence agent, Tommy was perfectly capable of sending Morse Code. But for tonight a simpler code system had been devised to cover all the necessary signals.

For openers, a single long buzz by Tommy would indicate that the enemy scuba divers had been spotted getting into position below the ship. The freighter *Sakamura* was docked to the pier directly opposite Tommy's vantage point.

Tommy Lee just happened to be a good enough scuba diver to be a pro at it. As a matter of fact, he occasionally filled in as an instructor or guide to pass the time while visiting his parents at their Hawaiian resort hotel. This was where he'd had most of his previous diving experience.

He'd done only a little diving as a teenager on the move with his family from city to city. During his Army furloughs in the Far East he became more interested in it, even to the point of ultimately wangling the chance for training at a military underwater demolition school after he convinced the brass that scuba skills would be useful on his assignment of investigating Saigon port thefts.

Tonight in these shallow and pollution-choked waters would be his greatest diving challenge of all.

When he first anchored his equipment to the dock, he swam stealthily underwater to the *Sakamura*. Using his flashlight freely under the hull, he checked for any indication that the Thunder and Lightning divers had jumped the gun and already removed the heroin cache. But the barnacle layer under the ship seemed reassuringly undisturbed. As he had expected, it was still too crowded along the waterfront for removal operations to have started tonight.

The crew of the Japanese freighter was rolling back and forth from shore leave during the first hour Tommy spent by dockside. But gradually they quieted down as most of the crew turned in.

Tommy put his diving mask in place and had himself a look at the bottom of the *Sakamura* from his vantage point every ten minutes or so. No diver crew had turned up early. It wasn't necessary to swim over to the boat or even turn on his flashlight to make sure the smugglers hadn't arrived yet.

The enemy scuba crew would have to be using their own searchlights to see what they were doing underneath the hull. Tommy would have a perfect homing beam when it was time to strike.

The minutes dragged by in cold, dark, and wetness. Tommy didn't bother attempting to relax with his usual zen meditation techniques. He just tried to hurry the hands of his underwater watch along and mentally go over the plan he and Lisa had hatched up earlier in the day.

Lisa had started by assuring him she could come up with fifty or sixty tough Mafia hoods, all dependable, level-headed, and good shots. But once Tommy had examined the photos and diagrams made in the morning by his East-West Investigations detectives, he realized that so many gunmen would only fall over each other and make the job more dangerous for all concerned. He made Lisa keep most of her force standing by for call-up in case of need for hot pursuit.

He insisted that only twenty-five of Lisa's men be assigned sniping positions around the docks and crew slots on the two fast motorboats waiting out in the bay. He assigned no more than ten of his own men to the job, all in carefully chosen positions mainly designed to protect his own rear while exposing the detectives to a minimum of danger.

As far as he was concerned, this was now the Mafia's fight, not Chinatown's. As he had told the Mafia council when all this started, a surprisingly few but fast-moving days ago ... He couldn't care less if the mob and the Thunder and Lightning gang slaughtered each other into oblivion. As a matter of fact, he'd prefer it.

Most of the daylight hours had been spent rounding up the complex assortment of marine equipment they would need to entrap the heroin smugglers successfully. There were also constant reassurances to Lisa and her aides that the plan was the best possible way to recover the submerged heroin containers for the Mafia.

That was one promise he never had any intention of keeping.

As midnight finally approached, Tommy gladly put on his mask for the last time and turned on the air tanks strapped to his back. He would remain underwater now until the smugglers came, keeping continuous watch for their telltale lights under the hull.

The T&L scuba team was late and Tommy started getting increasingly worried that Lo Sing hadn't properly understood what he overheard when tied up in the bunker.

But at just about ten minutes after midnight, Tommy observed the first bobbing lights going on underneath the wide, rounded bottom of the *Sakamura*. The divers may have been delayed en route but here they were now!

Tommy pressed the sender on his cable transmitter to indicate to the snipers at Lisa's command post on a warehouse rooftop overlooking the dock that the divers had arrived in position.

That was all he had to do until they got the heroin out.

There was only about eight feet of clear water between the hull of the *Sakamura* and the sticky muck of the harbor bottom. It was a crowded work area but there would apparently be enough space for what had to be done.

Four scuba divers were at work, with lights strapped around their heads. Tommy could observe the scene quite clearly from across about 150 feet of water, at the next dock.

The wide expanse of the *Sakamura's* bottom would pretty well keep the flashlight beams from escaping onto the adjoining water surface. Any stray illumination visible to a passer-by on pierside would doubtless be written off as merely reflections of the hillside city lights.

Tommy had wondered how the other scuba divers would be able to tell which of the hull plates to remove, what with all the barnacle layers collected during normal ocean travel obscuring any prior markings on the actual metal.

But the Thunder and Lightning had solved this problem with simple directness. One of the divers swam straight onward from the propeller screws of the ship with a light cord unreeling behind him. The string had been attached to the rudder assembly and it ran out at a pre-measured length. That was where the divers started scraping away the barnacle guck. In short order they had uncovered whatever signs they had been looking for and started to unscrew the corners of a hull plate close to the center of the ship. The measuring cord was just yanked off the rudder bar and went floating away.

The hull plate came off with the bolts remaining in the holes. A chain was attached to it from the inside and kept it floating just far enough to be out of the way.

One of the divers crawled into the hidden compartment and started shoving out yard-high metal cannisters connected by a line. The divers waiting outside the hatch blew up several medium-sized rubber tubes, each tube attached to its own air cartridge. The heroin cannisters were clamped to the tubes by their connecting lines and the inflated bags supplied just enough bouyancy to keep them floating exactly where placed. It was a neutral bouyancy that would allow the cumbersome chain of metal cans to be guided underwater with the flick of a finger.

Three of the divers started to put back the hull plate they had removed while the fourth kept a firm grip on the line of heroin cannisters. The entire operation had required well under five minutes.

And now there was no reason for Tommy Lee to hold off any longer.

He hit his cable transmitter key twice to indicate that he was going into action and ripped off the transmitter from the cables to sink into the muck. With the knife sheathed at his belt he first cut loose the rope anchoring him to the dock piling and then the lines holding back the bulky torpedo-like shape lashed between two pilings just below the water.

The weird looking projectile floated sluggishly on its own. Tommy slid behind a set of handlebar controls and punched a button. The machine's motor churned over a few times and growled into powerful life.

It was an underwater sled, propelled by motorized rotors that jetted out blasts of water behind. Devices like these were very expensive and not long out of the experimental stage. But you could purchase them at scuba supply shops if you searched long enough and Tommy had an entire detective agency at his disposal to run one down today.

Tommy joggled the handlebars and the sled zapped forward, angling slightly downward for the bottom of the *Sakamura*. This futuristic device covered underwater distance two or three times faster than any unmechanized scuba diver could ever hope to. It was Tommy's answer to how he could be sure of knocking out all the opposition divers no matter how many of them showed up.

He couldn't imagine that the T&L divers would give up the advantages of stealth and silence in this crowded harbor by using speedy motorized sleds of their own. But Tommy was close enough to his prey to have no need for stealth.

He rocketed across the short space of dark water to the *Sakamura* and was practically on top of the other divers' circle of illumination before they realized what was coming at them.

Of course the four divers under the *Sakamura* had looked up and stared into the darkness when they heard Tommy's engine start. But they couldn't see anything and for the first few seconds they had to assume the engine sound was merely a motorboat passing close overhead.

And by then, Tommy was upon them. He hadn't turned on the powerful searchlight built into the front of the sled. He didn't need to when he could home right in on the lights of the other divers.

His first target was naturally the diver holding onto the heroin containers. Tommy slammed the sled into him from the side, caving in his ribs and sending him flying headfirst into the hull. The heroin packs drifted lazily aside.

The impact against a human body only made the sled buck for a few seconds and Tommy was already bringing it around to run into the closest diver. He got this one full in the chest as the diver was trying to roll aside to open water. The diver was knocked back against the half-closed hatch and the exposed edge of the hull ripped open his wet-suit and sliced apart his air hoses. He wriggled away and made frantically for the surface.

Tommy's course carried him beyond the hull and he had to circle around to come back for the two final targets. He saw the divers gesturing and waving at each other. Then they abruptly turned off their headlights and the entire harbor bottom was plunged back into darkness.

Tommy responded by instantly switching on his own wide-angle bright sled headlight. The illumination picked out only one of the scuba pair still in action. It was the farthest diver and Tommy went for him with the sled.

The diver rolled and tumbled in an attempt to evade the charge of the fast-moving sled. Tommy crashed into his scuba tanks, popping open the connecting hoses because of the pressure from within the dented metal tubes.

The impact of metal on metal had given the sled its heaviest collision yet. Tommy fought to slew his vehicle around and come back to put the last remaining diver out of action.

He whipped the one-man craft along under the *Sakamura*'s hull, seeking his target. The knife coming out of the darkness from below almost thrust home into his groin.

The last of the enemy divers remaining operational had been the wiliest. He hid down at the very edge of the sticky harbor bottom muck until Tommy went by. Then he shot in from the rear to stab Tommy with his belt knife.

Most of Tommy's torso was shielded by the bottom of the sled, with only his legs dangling free to help maneuver. The attacking diver sought a crippling blow while the element of surprise was in his favor, rather than settling for a leg wound that would still leave Tommy mobile with his battering-ram sled.

But in the watery shadows, it was not easy to judge exact distances, as Tommy had already found out in his pursuits.

The knife struck upwards a few inches the wrong side of its moving target and deflected onto the metal bottom of the underwater sled.

Tommy reacted instantaneously when he heard the frightening scrape of the knife blade on the metallic skin beneath him. He went into an evasive side-roll at full speed, then plummeted down into a tricky circular dive that brought him around into position to ram the spot from where the diver had stabbed at him.

But Tommy's prey had taken off when the knife missed and now the scuba shape was slithering out below the edge of the hull.

Tommy halted his underwater sled and turned back to find the floating arrangement of heroin cannisters. He knew the last diver was finished now, just like the other three he had forced to surface at the sides of the *Sakamura*, because these shallow dockside waters would by now be brightly illuminated with searchlights from both the shore and patrolling nearby motorboats. To get out from under the smuggler ship, the disabled fleeing scuba divers would have to come close enough to the surface so that their outlines would be clearly visible to the waiting submachine gunners.

Tommy found the neutrally bouyant chain of dope cannisters floating lazily a few feet below the center of the hull. He throttled down his sled to the point where it remained unmoving in the water and swiftly tied the bobbing line of cannisters to a cleat on his vehicle. Cutting off a small length of the rope around his waist, he lashed the sled's control bars into a straight-ahead position.

Then he pressed a switch on a small black box which had been mounted on the instrument panel.

He pushed the throttle up to half-speed and cruised the sled out to the bow propellors of the ship. That was where he slid off the vehicle and let it carry its cargo of powdered death out toward the center of the bay at six feet below the water surface.

The bulk and shadows of the Japanese freighter made it impossible for the shore snipers to spot the sled as it moved away from them under improvised automatic pilot.

Tommy took advantage of the same cover to make his way out beyond the docked ship. It was only an escape to the sides of the vessel that led to the death traps of the searchlights and submachine gunners.

He went down as close to the harbor's muck bottom as he dared. He struck out to the right and didn't come up until he was well beyond the perimeter of flickering searchlights he could see playing over the surface.

By his underwater chronometer wristwatch, he'd kept watch on the amount of elapsed time since he switched on the black box on the sled. At precisely two minutes he surfaced just enough to poke his head out of the water.

He told himself he'd risked coming up in order to orient himself for returning to shore alongside a nearby deserted dock. But in reality he didn't want to miss the pleasure of seeing his final scheme in this operation working out.

At two minutes on the nose, there was a muffled underwater blast and a spectacularly high geyser of gray water spouted up in the bay.

The timing device in the black box had gone off, detonating the three sticks of dynamite Tommy had wrapped under the sled's dashboard. The heroin cans were now pulverized.

Tommy grinned and ducked back underwater to return to shore.

CHAPTER EIGHTEEN

Tommy came back to the surface again well under the pilings of a pier outside the boundaries of the searchlighted waterfront shooting gallery. It gave him a ringside seat to the finale of the battle.

He watched the gunshots still spattering the water along each side of the *Sakamura*. From his vantage point, he could spot one floating scuba diver's body and one spreading pool of blood. The others were probably hidden from him by the *Sakamura*.

The main action at this point was a gunfight between the motorboats out in the bay. The Mafia side had fielded three speedy launches with high intensity searchlights. One of the searchlights had been shot out. But the trio was efficiently boxing in the fast black motorboat that had brought the scuba divers into the harbor and was waiting for them to bring back the heroin.

There were a series of graceful sweeps and lunges accompanied by the scattering fire of automatic rifles as the Thunder and Lightning boat tried vainly to break past the three pursuers. The end came as might have been expected.

One of the three hunter boats swooped in behind the frantically darting T&L craft as it made a sudden reverse and a barrage of gunfire connected with its motor and gas tanks. The fleeing boat went up in a mushroom puff of crimson flame.

Although the sea battle was now over, there were still a couple of isolated pockets of firing on shore at the dockside. The Thunder and Lightning gang had infiltrated back-up parties into the pier area to cover any problems encountered by the divers.

But with the superior rooftop positions taken up by the Mafia snipers, and the brilliant illumination of the searchlights, there was no way the Chinese hoods could fight their way out of the trap. Most of the Mafia guns had been equipped with silencers to hold down the noise picked up outside this night-deserted South San Francisco harbor area. Mafia guards were at the pier gates to keep any unauthorized parties from coming in or out. Whoever of the *Sakamura* crew was aboard ship was very wisely keeping their heads down.

Tommy waited until the last gunshots had died away, indicating the downfall of the land resistance, before he climbed back up to the top of the pier. To signal his identity, he took out a long strip of bright red cloth pinned to his underwear and wound it all over his wet-suited torso. This was a prearranged sign for Lisa's men.

He strode unmolested down along the waterside to where a knot of about a dozen Mafioso gunmen were standing around. When he got closer to the group he found that Lisa was there amid the taller males. She was wearing what looked like a Paris-tailored G.I. combat suit of black suede with the form-hugging trousers tucked into shiny riding boots. She had a favorite weapon, a pump action shotgun, slung rakishly over her shoulder.

Lying on the concrete slabs in front of the victorious gunmen was a body, a Chinese corpse that had apparently just been killed and in a particularly unpleasant manner.

This body was different from the other gunned-down Thunder and Lightning bodies he'd already seen riddled with bullets along his walk from the dock.

This body had been stripped naked and most of the skin from its upper torso was peeled off into bleeding tatters. The poor bastard had been literally flayed alive to torture information out of him.

Tommy's face tightened in rage and revulsion. If he had been on the spot only a few minutes earlier he would never have permitted this atrocity to take place, not to a fellow Chinese or to any other human being. He noted the cloth placed loosely into the dead victim's mouth that would have cut off the volume of his otherwise ear-splitting screams but allowed him to speak when he gave in to the pain at last.

Lisa looked over at Tommy and said with infuriating perkiness, "Well, we took one alive to work on, for a change."

Tommy said disgustedly, "Did he tell you anything, or were kicks all you got out of it?"

"Toward the end he kept moaning about something that sounded like ... Daruma, the graveyard of the sea spirits. Does that mean anything to you?" Then Lisa snapped her fingers, the action seemingly bringing her out of her blood euphoria. "But that's not the most important thing right now, Lee," she said briskly. "Where's my heroin shipment?"

"Your heroin shipment?" Tommy blurted out in amazement. This bloodthirsty woman's greed and gall were truly incredible. "Did you happen to notice that first big explosion out in the bay, the underwater blast without any flame? You'll be sorry to hear that was your whole shipment of heroin."

"How did it happen?" Lisa's question was cold as ice.

Tommy glanced at the line-up of nearby gunmen and chose his lie. "While I was fighting with their scuba divers underwater.... One of them managed to shoot a speargun into the gas tank of my underwater sled and the watertight motor compartment caught on fire. I swam the hell out of there just before the blast went off."

Lisa looked at him intently. "I don't believe that story for a minute," she said. "You scuttled the sled yourself with a rigged bomb to keep my heroin from coming ashore. You simple-minded slant-eyed fool!"

She slapped Tommy in the face with her black-gloved hand as hard as she could and then came around for the backhand shot.

Tommy's cheek stung but he kept his expression impassive as she spun on her bootheel and flounced away from him, no doubt trying to decide if she should order him killed on the spot.

And then Tommy planted a stunning kick dead center on her suede-sheathed lovely ass and sent her flying over the side of the walkway to land in the dirty water fifteen feet below.

For a split-second, the tough Mafia gunmen were frozen into immobility by the sheer, incredible audacity of what Tommy had done to their leader.

And a split-second was all Tommy Lee ever needed. He moved in a blur of speed as he sprang at the nearest armed hoodlum and chopped down on the arm gripping an automatic rifle. Tommy grabbed the weapon in midair and crouched aiming at the rest of the mobsters as he shouted, "Freeze or I'll cut you in half."

Lisa had only yelped once as she went sprawling over into the water. She had too much pride to yell for help as she paddled to a dock piling. Tommy backed up and used his side vision to see her glaring up balefully at him.

He shouted down, "You're crazy if you think I'd deliver you even one speck of heroin to sell to kids or poor, crazed junkies.... And when you haul your ass on up out of there, you better get busy rounding up the rest of your army of tough boys waiting on stand-by. Because I happen to know what the unfortunate bastard you sliced up meant when he tried to tell you Thunder and Lightning were holed up on Daruma, the graveyard of sea spirits. If you're serious about wiping out the Thunder and Lightning, it's not even one A.M. yet and we've got plenty of time to hit them before dawn."

CHAPTER NINETEEN

By making all preparations at a breakneck speed and not stopping for any detailed explanations of why, Lisa Delmonico's full-sized fighting task force was ready to leave from its central assembly point a little after 3:30 a.m. that night.

The departure area was, appropriately enough, a syndicate-owned trucking company in Daly City. Activity of trucks and men at any hour of the night would be no suspicious occurrence.

There were just under a hundred Mafia thugs on hand, all armed to the teeth and many of them encased in the lightweight fiber bulletproof jackets that all sides in the current series of fights had been using so effectively.

A fleet of heavy trucks was set to take them to the final combat zone and the only thing left before they took off was for Tommy to explain to everybody exactly what was going on.

He was about to do just that in the trucking company's floodlit garage. A large-scale map of the San Francisco Bay Area was taped to the wall behind him and he pointed dramatically to a curving inlet at the northeasternmost extremity of the great bay.

"Port Arthur," he said. "That's where we're going. The prisoner you tortured tried to tell you to go to the graveyard of sea spirits. To Chinese tradition, ships are sea spirits. That's why they have eyes painted on the front of junks and all that sort of thing. Port Arthur is the Bay Area's biggest graveyard for dumping old ships that are waiting to go for scrap. It also happens to be where many of the Chinese illegal immigrants were landed from freighters earlier in the century, in hopes of avoiding immigration officials. Ever since I was a kid in Chinatown I've heard Port Arthur called the graveyard of sea spirits."

Lisa had changed into a new, dry combat outfit since her dunking. It was identical in cut with the previous costume, but this time in brown suede with matching boots. "What about Daruma?" she demanded. "He said that too."

"Daruma is the name of the monk who founded Zen Buddhism," said Tommy. "But in this context, I think it is also the name of a ship of Asiatic registry anchored in the Port Arthur graveyard. That's the ship they're operating their headquarters out of. If we had time, we could check the maritime records of the city and find out even the Daruma's exact location within the graveyard. But I think we can all see it would be better to go in on the gang tonight before they decide to change their base as a result of our ambushing their dope pickup successfully."

Tommy now handed around xeroxed copies of the photos of two young Chinese faces. "Try to keep those two in mind and yell for reinforcements if you come across them during the fighting. I have reason to believe they are the number one target ... gangleaders nicknamed Thunder and Lightning themselves."

The photos had been obtained by Tommy from his extensive files at East-West Investigations. The photo of Chooey, the former L.A. extortionist, had a scar drawn on it in the lightning slash Tommy had seen on his cheek. The other photo was of a smalltime Saigon waterfront punk named Shi Tan.

Shi Tan had achieved something of a reputation among the rats of Vietnamese criminality because of his rather astonishing boldness and cruelty ... as well as his virtuoso skill with an entire range of stolen U.S. Army portable cannons, the AR-70 grenade launcher, the lightweight howitzer, the mortar, and above all the clumsy but overwhelmingly lethal bazooka. It was believed that Shi Tan's foul and evil temper was fueled by constant pain from his napalm-withered right leg which caused him to limp.

It was this limp that Tommy spotted during the bazooka ambush that killed Bartlett Delmonico.

There was only one thing about the leadership of the Thunder and Lightning gang that still puzzled him now. How could these two mere punks, who'd never been known to succeed at planning anything beyond the meanest small-scale crimes, find the power and brains to put together such an unprecedentedly ruthless gang out of seemingly nothing but the most desperate misfits and castoffs?

Tommy finished his briefing by outlining the physical description of what the mobster force could expect to encounter at the Port Arthur ships' graveyard.

"There's nothing subtle about the line of attack," he said. "We're going to have to smash in and roll over them. If there was any time, we'd collect diagrams and photos and work out a whole lot of cute tricks. As it is, we've got some flare bombs to set off every once in a while so we can see what we're shooting at. And your friends will be cruising offshore in some nice big yachts in the likely event that you have to make an exit by swimming away from the cops that will eventually come driving in from the highway after enough ruckus is reported."

Port Arthur was pretty well abandoned by now, Tommy explained. Acre after acre of rotting old ships. Only a chain-link fence and barbed wire around the perimeter. Much of the dockage had been a military installation.

Port Arthur was last in the news as the secluded military port from which the maiming fire chemical, napalm, was shipped in bulk for the bombs being dropped on Vietnam. There were bitter war protest demonstrations outside the gates, many arrests, and mounting embarrassment by the authorities.

Ultimately the protestors and the increasingly blatant futility of the war brought around the majority of Americans and the Port Arthur napalm shipments quietly were discontinued. The district fell back into its prior disuse and obscurity.

Port Arthur was the perfect main hideout for a large criminal organization. It was vast and filled with nooks and crannies to keep out of sight in. Only a few watchmen would have to be bribed or otherwise gotten to for the gang to be able to operate out of here in total secrecy.

By now it was getting on to four a.m. and the caravan had to leave if it was going to make the trek northward across San Francisco and arrive at Port Arthur just before the first light of dawn.

It was an impressive enough caravan that rolled out of the lot, truck after truck crammed with men and weapons, cars strung out with walkie-talkies all along to guide and reconnoiter.

The procession had to spread out along the highway so it wouldn't look too obvious to any passing police cars nearing the end of their shifts. Tommy rode in the cab of the second truck in line. He had an automatic rifle and plenty of ammo clips. He'd decided to turn down one of the armor vests, he preferred to have all of his speed and agility on top for personal combat and would have to trust to luck to keep him away from stray bullets as his luck had done so often before.

Lisa was in one of the outrider cars keeping the caravan in radio communication. She and Tommy were keeping well away from each other by mutual consent at this point.

It was just about 4:40 when the caravan assembled in fighting formation at the roadside just beyond the Port Arthur exit of the freeway.

As a signal of flashing lights passed up and down the vehicle line, the procession rumbled forward. The lead truck, a huge mechanized beast with heavy steel grillwork protecting its front end, rolled along the outer fence to the locked main gate and kept right on going.

It didn't turn in until it came to a noticeably weakened area of the link fence, a section that sagged deeply between the iron holding-posts. Then the truck wheeled and slammed into the fence at forty miles an hour, snapping apart the rust-rotted links like confetti.

The truck that Tommy was riding in followed a bit to the side, widening the gap in the fence so more than one truck could enter at a time. The caravan moved ahead in the various available directions along the curving dockside. Without spreading themselves too thin, the trucks halted and the Mafia gunners started to leap out.

The one thing that Tommy's attack plan couldn't let happen was for the Thunder and Lightning defenders to simply lie in wait while mobsters advanced to a position where they could be blasted down in crossfire. He had to make sure the T&L desperadoes started shooting back, revealing their positions right away.

Out ahead of them, almost as far as the eye could see to the horizon, were the mothballed ships and barges of the Port Arthur floating graveyard. The desperate defenders could be taking aim right now from positions on any of these floating hulks.

But not if they were burned out!

The Mafia battalion had an ample supply of molotov cocktails and their first task was to heave these bottles of gasoline with the flaming wicks into boats throughout the graveyard.

In minutes there were thick flames and smoke going up to the steadily brightening gray pre-dawn sky all along the graveyard. Dim figures darted into view to escape the fires and their guns blasted down at the advancing attackers.

Bullets whipped back and forth with increasing intensity until before long there was a thunderous barrage of fire coming in at the mobsters from out in the bay. The first of the flare bombs went off overhead, illuminating clusters of scurrying figures on ship decks.

The full-scale battle was on!

Tommy hung back during this opening phase. He watched the emerging course of the gunfight from behind a stack of empty oil cans, not firing his own weapon yet. As far as he was concerned, his only mission was to find the actual lair of the two gangsters who called themselves

Thunder and Lightning. If those two escaped the carnage they could always re-form their deadly gang with new recruits, even if the bulk of their followers perished here.

And so Tommy carefully scanned the arc of gunfire hailing in on the Mafia men. It eventually seemed to him as if a disproportionate percentage of the bullets and projectiles were coming in from a shadowy hulk moored close offshore about midway in the graveyard. And a lot of the flak was heavier stuff than merely machine gun bullets. It was the kind of rockets and projectiles that Shi Tan, the Saigon bazooka whiz, might well be expected to be concentrating on.

Tommy kept his eyes on the boat he suspected as he waited for the next flare to go off. His vigil was not overlong and in the short-lived illumination of the flare he saw clearly that although the official registry name of the ship was covered by a suspiciously well-placed patch of rust, there were sloppy Chinese letters whitewashed along the side nearby.

And the Chinese characters spelled out Daruma!

Another excellent tactic, thought Tommy. It was unlikely that anyone who understood Chinese except the members of the Thunder and Lightning gang would come to Port Arthur these days. And the writing on the vessel meant nothing in itself, yet it would help the gang members to swiftly find their headquarters among all the similar wrecks in this graveyard.

So now Tommy's immediate problem was to find the best way to get through to the Daruma without getting shot down along the open piers.

He peered around the immediate dockside area and there by a stack of nearby crates he discovered just what he needed. It was a bright new yellow lift loader, perhaps the last working carrier vehicle in action for the Port Arthur skeleton maintenance crews.

He darted to the loader in a flash, jumped up into the driver's seat and was pleased to find that the key was in the ignition. He started the engine and worked the lever that raised the loading blade apparatus, stopping the metal plating just below eye-level so it would protect him effectively from frontal bullets in an excellent armor shield.

Then he stepped on the gas and skittered the machine around the edges of the dock area as fast as it would go.

He made it better than halfway to the Daruma before anyone in the opposition spotted him and opened up. Then the bullets were flying around him like a swarm of hornets. Too many of the shots came too close for comfort and pinged off the yellow side panel of the loader as Tommy crouched behind the protective shell and drove forward hunched over the wheel.

Not a moment too soon, he passed behind the shelter of a dockside shed. The opposition marksmen had gotten him pretty well zeroed in by now.

But Tommy's brief sense of relief was over instantly as a trio of Thunder and Lightning riflemen came charging out of the shed at him.

Tommy aimed his machine right at the trio and bore down on them as their automatic rifle bursts clanged off his blade shield. He clobbered two of them right through the shed wall before he backed off and the third went leaping wildly into the water below the pier to escape.

Tommy drove the loader out past the far side of the shed. The Daruma was dead ahead now, he was close enough for the first time to see that the ship was tied alongside a rickety wooden railing rather than moored in the bay as he had originally thought.

But the marksmen waiting on the deck had been poised for the moment that Tommy poked the loader's snout in their direction. They blasted away at him as Tommy hustled the little vehicle onto the wobbly wooden railing dock. He'd be in their range too long if he tried to turn around and get back behind his own lines.

If it wasn't for the shield effect of the loader blades, he would never have made it. He knew his only chance was to work his way close enough to the ship so that he was inside their angle of fire. They certainly couldn't stand up at the deck rails and shoot straight down at him, not unless they wanted to offer themselves as Mafia sharpshooter targets.

The wooden slats buckled under the loader's wheels

and he could smell gas leaking from a puncture in the gas tank. He had to figure a way onto the ship on the run, and within the next few seconds.

Just then a rocket shell came slamming just over the top of the loader to gouge a huge hole into the boardwalk pier behind Tommy. Shi Tan had been called into the fray and he'd have the range down pat on his next round.

But now Tommy saw the wide rectangular hole in the side of the ship coming up. A cargo hatch and his ticket aboard the Daruma. He jumped out of the trundling loader's side away from the ship and let it proceed down the end of the boardwalk and over into the water, drawing gunfire after it all the way.

As for Tommy, he leaped into the cargo hatch the instant the loader went by and scrambled a few steps across the sloshing bilge to get out of the backlight coming into the cargo hold from the hatchway.

Then he didn't move at all for almost two minutes while he let his eyes get used to the darkness. He saw the obvious way out to the upper decks first, steep metal stairs to a corridor above. It took considerably more observation to discover that there were a series of rungs in the wall which led up past a set of gaping portholes whose glass was long gone.

He chose the rungs, the corridor above the stairs looked too much like a set-up. He moved slowly and carefully across the damp junk on the rotting floor of the hold. The few sounds he made were muffled by the regular lapping of waves in the bay.

He climbed stealthily up the rungs, varying the rhythm of his movements in order to throw off the perceptions of anybody around with especially good hearing. When he finally got almost abreast of the open portholes he halted and silently removed the top bullet from one of the spare ammunition clips on his belt. He tossed the bullet a short diagonal distance across the hold into the shadowy opening of the corridor at the top of the stairs.

The tiny clink of the bullet's landing was instantly answered by a mighty burst of submachine gun fire.

Tommy used the moment of misdirection to pop one

glance out of the porthole and, seeing the route was clear, slipped quickly out onto an open deck with his own submachine gun in firing position.

Even as the firing stopped from inside the ambush corridor, two T&L gangsters came around some steps onto the deck section where Tommy crouched. He had no choice but to squeeze his trigger and mow them down before they did the same to him.

He knew even as he fired that his bullets announced to every enemy aboard that he was on deck. In the tense silence after the shooting he caught the patter of rubber-soled feet running up somewhere behind him and whirled about. He was just in time to see Chooey, the lightning scar livid on his cheek, poking the barrel of a rifle over a railing above him.

He fired off a burst and Chooey ducked back out of sight.

Tommy knew he couldn't stay where he was any longer or they'd pick him off. A few feet away was a half-open hatch door leading into an abandoned cabin. He kicked it open and darted inside.

He went out through another hatchway at the far end of the room and came out in an interior corridor. Footsteps were racing behind into the room he had just left. Tommy kept moving ahead.

He found himself passing through a strange maze of interconnected rooms and passageways. Some of the cubicles were rusty and long dead, while others had electric lights and were fixed up into comfortable bunk rooms.

The sound of pursuit behind him faded and he began to advance more cautiously. He moved through chambers of stored supplies, food and weapons mostly. He started to think perhaps he heard some new sly sounds not too far off, pattering feet that halted when his own steps halted.

But each time he turned around to look behind him he could see nothing in the shadows. Moving even more warily now, he began to make his way down a corridor that was actually an open-sided metal gangplank that ran across the top of the cavernous engine room.

Halfway across the gangplank, the clang of someone leaping onto the metal walkway right behind him rang out like a bell of doom.

Tommy whirled around in an instantaneous blur of speed. Hatchet Wang had just vaulted over the side railing from some ladderway out of the depths of the engine room. His deadly little axe was at the top of the upswing before slashing down to split Tommy's skull open.

Tommy continued to pivot backwards and as he got himself leaning his shoulder into Wang's chest so his body passed beyond the impact arc of Wang's extended arm, he was also jamming the solid wooden butt of his automatic rifle into the pit of Wang's stomach as hard as he had ever hit anything in his life.

The breath whooshed out of Wang, his arms and legs spreadeagled and he went flying over the waist-high railing still clutching his hatchet. The sound of his crash into the bottom of the engine room echoed upward from far below.

The whole thing was over in fractions of a second as Tommy brought off the only maneuver that could have possibly saved his life.

He moved on through some more of the comfortable bunk cabins and found himself in a dead-end corridor with only one closed hatch leading out.

Bracing himself, he kicked open the hatchdoor and suddenly found himself face to face with at least a dozen dark-clothed tall Chinese with unusual translucent-pale complexions pointing submachine guns at him!

Tommy barely stopped his finger from squeezing a barrage of gunfire around the room as he suddenly realized he had stepped into a bizarre hall of mirrors.

He was seeing a circle of reflections of himself as he closed the hatch behind him. The floor of the large chamber was lined with mattresses surmounted by mounds of pillows. Tommy realized this weird room had to be some kind of orgy place, that was its only possible use.

And then he heard footsteps making no effort to silence

themselves. In a flash there was another image superimposed on the mirrors with him.

It was the reflection of the gun-wielding hoodlum with the hideous lightning scar, Chooey....

"I knew you'd have to pass through our little playroom once you got into the cabin deck," laughed the dozen Chooeys. "All the corridors pass through here to get through the other side. So I just had to intercept you."

Tommy said, "So bring on the chicks and we'll have a party in your swinging pad here."

"This is the party where you get killed," said Chooey. "I know how these mirrors are set up and you don't. I know where the real Tommy Lee is standing. But you don't know where is the real corridor I just walked down and which is the reflection. Go ahead, sucker, shoot up a couple of mirrors. Maybe you'll get lucky and hit something besides a reflection ... even though the odds are way against you."

Tommy's eyes darted rapidly around the room while Chooey laughed uproariously at his plight. Chooey probably wouldn't have been laughing if he realized that Tommy was simply determining how many light fixtures he would have to shoot out in order to plunge the entire room into darkness. And in a dark room, Tommy was perfectly happy to take on anybody and all the friends they might want to bring along.

But right then a whole section of mirror panels came rolling aside on coasters and Shi Tan, the other half of the Thunder and Lightning leader team, came lurching and limping in with his bazooka bobbing awkwardly on his shoulder.

"I won't let him get you, Lightning," Shi Tan shrieked as his bazooka belched flame and a rocket shell in the direction of Tommy's nearest mirror-image.

Tommy and all his reflections dived for the floor and burrowed into a pile of orgy pillows. He did not come out from the far end of the pillow mound until the countless razor slivers of mirror glass sent flying by the bazooka shell stopped ripping into the fabric stuffing that shielded him.

What Tommy saw when he looked around the room again was a lot of shattered mirrors and Shi Tan, with his bazooka thrown away, tenderly cradling the body of Chooey in his arms. A long and extremely nasty shard of mirror glass was sticking out of Chooey's eye as he lay there unmoving. The glass dagger must have penetrated deep into Chooey's brain.

Shi Tan burst into sobs and kissed Chooey's dead lips passionately. He moaned, "Oh my darling Lightning, your Thunder doesn't want to live without you. Alone we were nothing. But when we came together and gave each other everything . . . then we were able to accomplish everything we'd ever dreamed of."

Only then did Shi Tan seem to realize that Tommy was standing right over him with a submachine gun. He began to scrabble for a pistol holstered at his belt. "I'll kill you," he shouted wildly at Tommy. "You destroyed everything for me."

"Stop, Shi Tan," Tommy yelled back. "You make one more move for that gun and I'll blow you apart."

A sudden moment of lucidity seemed to return to the napalm-crippled Saigon hoodlum who'd taken the name of Thunder. He glared coldly at Tommy without moving and then, apparently making his final decision, he started to pull his gun out of the holster.

Tommy emptied the submachine gun's clip into him.

He'd fought Thunder and Lightning to the death and they died unfolding the secret of their reckless power. Somehow their clandestine homosexual love had turned the scarred Chooey and the crippled Shi Tan into a weird siamese twin of criminal genius. Together they fed off each other and rose to greater cleverness, toughness, and bravado than either had imagined being as separate individuals.

With their leaders gone, the Thunder and Lightning gang would fall apart into a motley rabble, even those who survived the gunfight outside.

Tommy had achieved all he set out to do for the united tong council of San Francisco's Chinatown community.

Looking about the ruins left by the shattered mirror

frames, he saw an open trapdoor with a ladder leading downward. So the unholy lovers had an escape route in case of big trouble. Tommy put another clip into his weapon and set off down the ladder.

The rungs ended at a small passageway cut into the side of the ship. The passage emptied underneath the adjoining jetty and hidden among the pilings was a small motorboat.

Tommy cut loose the lines, pulled the starter cable on the outboard and nudged the little boat past the pilings. Then he took off for the center of the bay in the first pink horizon light of dawn.

Behind him, Lisa Delmonico's Mafia killers and the vicious renegades of the Thunder and Lightning gang were still raining bullets back and forth. Tommy Lee wished them all the luck they needed for murdering each other.

INTRODUCING TWO NEW, EXCITING, ACTION-PACKED ADVENTURE SERIES OF SPECIAL INTEREST TO KUNG-FU FANS

Meet Sloane

Eastern martial arts and the raw violence of the American West join in the most dynamic Kung-Fu Western Series ever written.

Sloane #1:
THE MAN WITH THE IRON FISTS
by Steve Lee $1.25

Sloane—the toughest, deadliest, Kung-Fu warrior of the Old West—in a no-holds-barred, electrifying new series of violence and adventure.

Sloane #2:
A FISTFUL OF HATE
by Steve Lee $1.25

Flying fists and lethal feet match themselves against blazing guns as Sloane rips a bloody path through Western trails.

Meet John Crown

A fast moving blend of cops and Kung-Fu in the exotic setting of modern Hong Kong.

Crown #1:
THE SWEET AND SOUR KILL
by Terry Harknett $1.25

Hong Kong—city of sins, slums, and splendor. John Crown—hard-drinking, hard-loving, hard-fighting and the toughest cop in the Far East.

ORDER HERE:
PINNACLE BOOKS, 275 Madison Avenue, New York, N.Y. 10016

Please send me _____P484 SLOANE #1 _____P526 SLOANE #2 _____P503 CROWN #1
Enclosed is my check or money order.

_____Check here if you wish to receive our catalog regularly

PB-22

ALL NEW DYNAMITE SERIES
THE DESTROYER
by Richard Sapir & Warren Murphy

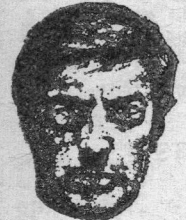

CURE, the world's most secret crime-fighting organization created the perfect weapon—Remo Williams—man programmed to become a cold, calculating death machine. The super man of the 70s!

Order	#	Title	Book No.	Price
	1	Created, The Destroyer	P361	$1.25
	2	Death Check	P362	$1.25
	3	Chinese Puzzle	P363	$1.25
	4	Mafia Fix	P364	$1.25
	5	Dr. Quake	P365	$1.25
	6	Death Therapy	P366	$1.25
	7	Union Bust	P367	$1.25
	8	Summit Chase	P368	$1.25
	9	Murder's Shield	P369	$1.25
	10	Terror Squad	P370	$1.25
	11	Kill or Cure	P371	$1.25
	12	Slave Safari	P372	$1.25
	13	Acid Rock	P373	$1.25
	14	Judgment Day	P303	$1.25
	15	Murder Ward	P331	$1.25
	16	Oil Slick	P418	$1.25
	17	Last War Dance	P435	$1.25
	18	Funny Money	P538	$1.25
	19	Holy Terror	P640	$1.25
	20	Assassins Play-Off	P708	$1.25
	21	Deadly Seeds	P760	$1.25
	22	Brain Drain	P805	$1.25
	23	Child's Play	P842	$1.25
	24	King's Curse	P879	$1.25

TO ORDER
Please check the space next to the book/s you want, send this order form together with your check or money order, include the price of the book/s and 25¢ for handling and mailing to:
PINNACLE BOOKS, INC. / P.O. BOX 4347
Grand Central Station / New York, N.Y. 10017
☐ CHECK HERE IF YOU WANT A FREE CATALOG
I have enclosed $_____ check _____ or money order _____ as payment in full. No C.O.D.'s.

Name_____

Address_____

City_____ State_____ Zip_____
(Please allow time for delivery.)

PB-39

the Executioner

The gutsiest, most exciting hero in years. Imagine a guy at war with the Godfather and all his Mafioso relatives! He's rough, he's deadly, he's a law unto himself — nothing and nobody stops him!

THE EXECUTIONER SERIES by DON PENDLETON

Order		Title	Book #	Price
	# 1	WAR AGAINST THE MAFIA	P401	$1.25
	# 2	DEATH SQUAD	P402	$1.25
	# 3	BATTLE MASK	P403	$1.25
	# 4	MIAMI MASSACRE	P404	$1.25
	# 5	CONTINENTAL CONTRACT	P405	$1.25
	# 6	ASSAULT ON SOHO	P406	$1.25
	# 7	NIGHTMARE IN NEW YORK	P407	$1.25
	# 8	CHICAGO WIPEOUT	P408	$1.25
	# 9	VEGAS VENDETTA	P409	$1.25
	#10	CARIBBEAN KILL	P410	$1.25
	#11	CALIFORNIA HIT	P411	$1.25
	#12	BOSTON BLITZ	P412	$1.25
	#13	WASHINGTON I.O.U.	P413	$1.25
	#14	SAN DIEGO SIEGE	P414	$1.25
	#15	PANIC IN PHILLY	P415	$1.25
	#16	SICILIAN SLAUGHTER	P552	$1.25
	#17	JERSEY GUNS	P328	$1.25
	#18	TEXAS STORM	P353	$1.25
	#19	DETROIT DEATHWATCH	P419	$1.25
	#20	NEW ORLEANS KNOCKOUT	P475	$1.25
	#21	FIREBASE SEATTLE	P499	$1.25
	#22	HAWAIIAN HELLGROUND	P625	$1.25
	#23	ST. LOUIS SHOWDOWN	P687	$1.25
	#24	CANADIAN CRISIS	P779	$1.25
	#25	COLORADO KILL-ZONE	P824	$1.25
	#26	ACAPULCO RAMPAGE	P868	$1.25

TO ORDER
Please check the space next to the book/s you want, send this order form together with your check or money order, include the price of the book/s and 25¢ for handling and mailing to:
PINNACLE BOOKS, INC. / P.O. BOX 4347
Grand Central Station / New York, N.Y. 10017
☐ CHECK HERE IF YOU WANT A FREE CATALOG
I have enclosed $_____check_____or money order_____
as payment in full. No C.O.D.'s.

Name_____

Address_____

City_____State_____Zip_____
(Please allow time for delivery)   PB-38